SOLD

PATRICIA McCORMICK

HYPERION PAPERBACKS
New York

Printed in the United States of America
First Hyperion Paperbacks edition, 2008
20 19 18 17 16 15 14 13 12 11
Library of Congress Cataloging-in-Publication Data on file.
ISBN-13: 978-0-7868-5172-0
ISBN-10: 0-7868-5172-4
V475-2873-0-13179

This book is set in Kennerley.
Designed by Ellice M. Lee
Visit www.hyperionteens.com

FOR PAUL

A TIN ROOF

One more rainy season and our roof will be gone, says Ama.

My mother is standing on a log ladder, inspecting the thatch, and I am on the ground, handing the laundry up to her so it can bake dry in the afternoon sun. There are no clouds in sight. No hint of rain, no chance of it, for weeks.

There is no use in telling Ama this, though. She is looking down the mountain at the rice terraces that descend, step by step, to the village below, at the neighbors' tin roofs winking cruelly back at her.

A tin roof means that the family has a father who doesn't gamble away the landlord's money playing cards in the tea shop. A tin roof means the family has a son working at the brick kiln in the city. A tin roof means that when the rains come, the fire stays lit and the baby stays healthy.

"Let me go to the city," I say. "I can work for a rich family like Gita does, and send my wages home to you."

Ama strokes my cheek, the skin of her work-worn hand as rough as the tongue of a newborn goat. "Lakshmi, my child," she says. "You must stay in school, no matter what your stepfather says."

Lately, I want to tell her, my stepfather looks at me the same way he looks at the cucumbers I'm growing in front of our hut. He flicks the ash from his cigarette and squints. "You had better get a good price for them," he says.

When he looks, he sees cigarettes and rice beer, a new vest for himself.

I see a tin roof.

BEFORE GITA LEFT

We drew squares in the dusty path between our huts and played the hopping-on-one-leg game. We brushed each other's hair a hundred strokes and dreamed of names for our sons and daughters. We pinched our noses shut whenever the headman's wife passed by, recalling the time she broke wind strutting past us at the village spring.

We rubbed the rough-edged notch in the school bench for good luck before a recitation. We threw mud at each other during the long afternoons stooped over in the paddies, and wept with laughter when one of Gita's mud pies hit her haughty older sister in the back of the head.

And in the fall, when the goatherds came down from the Himalayan meadows, we hid in the elephant grass to catch sight of Krishna, the boy with sleepy cat eyes, the one I am promised to in marriage.

Now that Gita is gone, to work as a maid for a wealthy woman in the city, her family has a tiny glass sun that hangs from a wire in the middle of their ceiling, a new set of pots for Gita's mother, a pair of spectacles for her father, a brocaded wedding dress for her older sister, and school fees for her little brother.

Inside Gita's family's hut, it is daytime at night.
But for me, it feels like nighttime even in the brightest sun
without my friend.

THE NEW STUDENT

Each morning as I go about my chores—straining the rice water, grinding the spices, sweeping the yard—my little black-and-white speckled goat, Tali, follows at my heels.

"That silly goat," Ama says. "She thinks you are her mother."

Tali nudges her head into the palm of my hand and bleats in agreement. And so I teach her what I know.

I wipe the hard mud floor with a rag soaked in dung water and explain: "This will keep our hut cool and free from evil spirits." I show her how I lash a water jug to the basket on my back, not spilling a drop on the steep climb up from the village spring. And when I brush my teeth with a twig from the neem tree, Tali copies me, nibbling her twig as solemn as a monk.

When it's time for me to go to school, I make her a bed of straw in a sunny corner of the porch. I kiss her between the ears and tell her I'll be home in time for the midday meal.

She presses her moist pink nose into the pocket of my skirt, searching for a bit of stowaway grain, then settles down, a jumble of elbows and knees, burrowing into the straw to nap.

"What a funny animal," Ama says. "She thinks she is a person." Ama must be right, because one day last week when I was sitting in the schoolroom, I heard the tinkling of her bell and looked up and saw my little speckled goat wandering around the school yard, bleating in despair.

When finally she spotted me through the window, she *bahhed* with wounded pride, indignant at being left behind. She marched across the yard, propped her hooves up on the windowsill, and looked in with keen and curious eyes as the teacher finished the lesson.

When school was over and we climbed the hill toward home, Tali trotted ahead, her stubby tail held high.

"Next week," I promised her, "we will work on our spelling."

SOMETHING BEAUTIFUL

In the morning, Ama bends down to stir the kitchen fire and to plait my hair before I go to school. All day, as she trudges up and down the mountain, a heavy basket braced on her back and held fast by a rope around her brow, she is bent under the weight of her burden.

And at night, as she serves my stepfather his dinner, she kneels at his feet.

Even when she is standing upright to scan the sky for rain clouds, my ama's back is stooped.

The people who live on our mountain, a cluster of red mud huts clinging to the slope, worship the goddess who lives there, on the swallow-tailed peak. They pray to the goddess whose brow is fierce and noble, whose breast is broad and bountiful, whose snowy skirts spread wide above us.

She is beautiful, mighty, and magnificent.

But my ama, with her crow-black hair braided with bits of red rag and beads, her cinnamon skin, and her ears hung with the joyful noise of tinkling gold, is, to me, more lovely.

And her slender back, which bears our troubles—and all our hopes—is more beautiful still.

THE DIFFERENCE BETWEEN A SON AND A DAUGHTER

My stepfather's arm is a withered and useless thing. Broken as a child when there was no money for a doctor, his poor mangled limb pains him during the rainy months and gives him great shame.

Most of the men his age leave home for months at a time, taking jobs at factories or on work crews far away. But no one, he says, will hire a one-armed man. And so he oils his hair, puts on his vest and a wristwatch that stopped telling time long ago, and goes up the hill each day to play cards, talk politics, and drink tea with the old men.

Ama says we are lucky we have a man at all. She says I am to honor and praise him, respect and thank him for taking us in after my father died.

And so I act the part of the dutiful daughter. I bring him his tea in the morning and rub his feet at night. I pretend I do not hear him joining in the laughter when the men at the tea shop joke about the difference between fathering a son and marrying off a daughter.

A son will always be a son, they say. But a girl is like a goat. Good as long as she gives you milk and butter. But not worth crying over when it's time to make a stew.

BEYOND THE HIMALAYAS

At dawn, our hut, perched high on the mountainside, is already torched with sunlight, while the village below remains cloaked in the mountain's long purple shadow until midmorning.

By midday, the tawny fields will be dotted with the cheerful dresses of the women, red as the poinsettias that lace the windy footpaths. Napping babies will sway in wicker baskets, and lizards will sun themselves outside their holes.

In the evening, the brilliant yellow pumpkin blossoms will close, drunk on sunshine, while the milky white jasmine will open their slender throats and sip the chill Himalayan air.

At night, low hearths will send up wispy curls of smoke fragrant with a dozen dinners, and darkness will clothe the land.

Except on nights when the moon is full. On those nights, the hillside and the valley below are bathed in a magical white light, the glow of the perpetual snows that blanket the mountaintops. On those nights I lie restless in the sleeping loft, wondering what the world is like beyond my mountain home.

CALENDAR

At school there is a calendar, where my young, moonfaced teacher marks off the days with a red crayon.

On the mountain we mark time by women's work and women's woes.

In the cold months, the women climb high up the mountain's spine to scavenge for firewood. They take food from their bowls, feed it to their children, and silence their own churning stomachs.

This is the season when the women bury the children who die of fever.

In the dry months, the women collect basketfuls of dung and pat them into cakes to harden in the sun, making precious fuel for the dinner fire. They tie rags around their children's eyes to shield them from the dust blowing up from the empty riverbed.

This is the season when they bury the children who die from the coughing disease.

In the rainy months, they patch the crumbling mud walls of their huts and keep the fire going so that yesterday's gruel can be stretched to make tomorrow's dinner. They watch the river turn into a thundering beast. They pick leeches from their children's feet and give them tea to ward off the loose-bowel disease.

This is the season when they bury the children who cannot be carried to the doctor on the other side of that river.

In the cool months, they prepare special food for the festivals. They make rice beer for the men and listen to them argue politics. They teach the children who have survived the seasons to make back-to-school ink from the blue-black juice of the marking nut tree.

This is also the season when the women drink the blue-black juice of the marking nut tree to do away with the babies in their wombs—the ones who would be born only to be buried next season.

ANOTHER CALENDAR

According to the number of notches in Ama's wedding trunk, she is thirty-one and I am thirteen. If my baby brother lives through the festival season, Ama will carve a notch for him.

Four other babies were born between me and my brother. There are no notches for them.

CONFESSION

Each of my cucumbers has a name.

There is the tiny one, Muthi, which means "size of a handful." Muthi gets the first drink of the day.

Nearby is Yeti, the biggest one, named for the hairy snow monster. Yeti grows so fat, little Muthi cowers under a nearby leaf in fear and awe.

There is Ananta, the one shaped like a snake; and Bajai, the gnarled grandmother of the group; Vishnu, as sleek as rain; and Naazma, the ugly one, named for the headman's wife.

There is one named for my hen and three for her chicks, one for Gita, and one for Ganesh, the elephant god, remover of obstacles.

I treat them all as my children.

But sometimes, if my water jug runs low, I scrimp a bit on Naazma.

FIRST BLOOD

I awoke today—before even the hen had begun to stir—
aware of a change in myself.

For days I have sensed a ripening in my body, a tender, achy,
feeling unlike anything I've felt before. And even before I go
to the privy to check, I know that I have gotten my first blood.

Ama is delighted by my news and sets about making the
arrangements for my confinement.

"You must stay out of sight for seven days," she says. "Even
the sun cannot see you until you've been purified."

Before the day can begin, Ama hurries me off to the goat
shed, where I will spend the week shut away from the world.

"Don't come out for any reason," she says. "If you must use
the privy, cover your face and head with your shawl.

"At night," she says, "when your stepfather has gone out and
the baby has gone to sleep, I will return. And then I will tell
you everything you need to know."

EVERYTHING I NEED TO KNOW

Before today, Ama says, you could run as free as a leaf in
the wind.

Now, she says, you must carry yourself with modesty, bow
your head in the presence of men, and cover yourself with
your shawl.

Never look a man in the eye.
Never allow yourself to be alone with a man who is not family.
And never look at growing pumpkins or cucumbers when
you are bleeding.
Otherwise they will rot.

Once you are married, she says, you must eat your meal only
after your husband has had his fill. Then you may have what
remains.

If he burps at the end of the meal, it is a sign that you have
pleased him.

If he turns to you in the night, you must give yourself to him,
in the hopes that you will bear him a son.

If you have a son, feed him at your breast until he is four.

If you have a daughter, feed her at your breast for just a

season, so that your blood will start again and you can try once more to bear a son.

If your husband asks you to wash his feet, you must do as he says, then put a bit of the water in your mouth.

I ask Ama why. "Why," I say, "must women suffer so?"

"This has always been our fate," she says.
"Simply to endure," she says, "is to triumph."

WAITING AND WATCHING

For seven days and seven nights, I lie in the darkness of the goat shed dreaming of my future. I bury my nose in Tali's fur and breathe in the smell of her—sweet green shoots of grass, afternoon sun, and mountain dirt—and imagine my life with Krishna.

Ama says that I must wait until next year when she visits the astrologer to fix a date for our wedding. But I would go live with him in the mountains tomorrow if I could.

We could eat riverweed and drink snowmelt and sleep under the silver-white light of the mountain. And someday, we could hang a cloth from a tree branch and put our baby in it. And she would sleep with the bleating of the goats as her only lullaby.

Until then, I will content myself with watching him.

I was watching when he won a footrace against the fastest boy in the village. And I was there the day he put a lizard in the teacher's teacup. I was at the village fountain when the other boys teased him for hauling water for his mother. And I was peeking out from around the corner of Bajai Sita's store the time he smoked his first cigarette and he coughed until he cried.

Krishna is shy when he passes me in the village, his sleepy cat eyes fixed on the ground in front of his feet.

But I think, perhaps, that he has been watching me, too.

ANNOUNCING THE DRY SEASON

The wind that blows up from the plains is called the *loo.*

It churns all day, hot and restless, throwing handfuls of dirt
into the air and making the water in my mouth turn to mud.

It cries all night, too, blowing its feverish breath through
the cracks in our walls, speaking its name again and again.
"*Loo,*" it wails, announcing itself all over the land.
"*Looooooo . . .*"

FIFTY DAYS WITHOUT RAIN

The leaves on my cucumbers are edged in brown, and Ama and I must each make twenty trips down the mountain to the village spring, waiting our turn to bring water up to the rice paddy.

My stepfather dozes in the shade, wearing nothing but a loincloth, too hot even to climb the hill to his card game.

The baby wears nothing at all.

Even the lizards lie gasping in the heat.

MAKING DO

Today the village headmen announced that they will ration water.
Tonight Ama and I scrub the cooking vessels clean with a mixture of earth and ash.

SIXTY DAYS WITHOUT RAIN

The rice plants are brown and parched, coated in dust. The wind rips the weakest of them out by the roots and tosses them off the mountainside.

Tali creeps over to the creek bed and rests her chin on the bank, her tongue searching for water that isn't there.

The baby's eyes are caked with dirt. He cries without fury. He cries without tears.

MAYBE TOMORROW

Today, like yesterday, and the day before, and the day before that, the sky is deadly blue.

Today, like each day before, the water in the rice paddy drops a little farther, and the plants hang their heads a little lower.

I watch as Ama makes an offering of marigold petals, red kumkum powder, and a few precious bits of rice to her goddess, praying for rain. But the only water that falls comes from Ama's eyes.

I go back to mopping the baby's face with a damp rag. As Ama goes past, I touch the hem of her skirt.

"Maybe tomorrow, Ama," I say.

My stepfather rises from his cot. "If the rains don't come soon," he says to my mother, "you will have to sell your earrings."

Yesterday, or the day before, or the day before that, Ama would have said, "Never." She would have said, "Those are for Lakshmi. They are her dowry."

But today she hangs her head like the paddy plants and says, "Maybe tomorrow."

WHAT IS MISSING

The next morning, I rise before the sun has climbed over the mountain and walk down to the village spring, my feet making tiny dust storms with each step.

When I get home, I notice that my stepfather's cot is empty—he's behind the hut, I expect, in the privy. Before he can return to start calling out orders, I sneak over to my garden plot, with the first of the day's water for my thirsty cucumbers. I lift the leaf where Muthi likes to hide.

But all I see is a stem, looking surprised, lonely.

Ananta the snake, and even big fat Yeti are also missing, as are all the others.

I understand slowly, then all at once, that my stepfather has taken my cucumbers to Bajai Sita, the old trader woman, and sold them. I understand, too, why his cot is empty. Most likely, he has spent the night gambling—and losing—at the tea shop.

I know this is so when Ama comes out of the hut and does not meet my eye.

She takes the urn from my hands, pours the water over the few rice plants that remain. We strap the jugs to our backs, head down toward the spring, and do not speak of what is missing.

WHEN THE RAIN CAME

I smelled the rain before it fell.

I felt the air grow heavy like roti dough and saw the leaves of the eucalyptus tree turn their silvery undersides up to greet it.

The first few droplets vanished in the dust. Then bigger drops fell, fat and ripe, exploding the earth.

Ama came out of the house, pulling her shawl over her head. Then, slowly, she lifted the folds of fabric away from her brow and, like the leaves of the eucalyptus tree, raised her waiting face toward heaven.

I ran across the yard, released Tali from her wooden peg, and led her to the creek bed, her tongue unwilling to trust. Then, little by little, a trickle of muddy water came hopping down the gully.

Tali lapped and snuffled and snorted and sneezed and drank herself silly, her bony sides billowing with water.

I shut my eyes tight, letting the tears that had been gathering there finally spill down my cheeks, where they could hide inside the rain.

STRANGE MUSIC

I awake the next day to a forgotten sound.

Even before the rest of us have stirred, Ama has spread pots and pitchers around the floor of the hut to catch the water seeping in through the gaps in our roof.

I climb down from the sleeping loft, stir the fire, and brew a new pot of tea from yesterday's leaves, not daring to meet Ama's eyes, each drip a reminder of the tin roof we don't have.

Then the baby awakes. And with each drip
and *plink*
and *plop*
and *ping*
he laughs and claps his hands.
Each drip new.
Each *plink*
and *plop*
and *ping*
fresh and strange and musical to his tiny ears.

Ama wipes her hands on her apron, looks up at our old roof with new eyes, and lifts the baby from his basket. She twirls him in the air, her skirts flying around her ankles the way the clouds swirl around the mountain cap—her laughter fresh and strange and musical to my ears.

MAYBE

That night, after my stepfather leaves for the tea shop and the baby falls asleep, Ama reaches behind a big urn for a smaller one. She feels around behind that urn for an even smaller one, reaches inside, and pulls out a handful of maize.

"I set this aside in the dry months," she says, "for a night"—she gestures to the falling rain outside—"like tonight."

She pours the kernels into the skillet, sits back on her heels, and we watch as they burst into flower. I offer to share the little bowl of popcorn with her, but Ama has another surprise in store.

She unwinds the fabric at her waist and pulls out one of my stepfather's precious cigarettes, and I see, in that moment, the mischievous girl she was at my age.

We sit together, each savoring our secret treats and dreaming of the days after the monsoon.

"The first thing we'll do," I say, "is patch the roof."

"No, child," she says, solemnly blowing smoke in the air. "First, we'll offer thanks to the goddess. Then we'll mend the roof."

She inhales. "Perhaps this year we can beg some new thatch

from the landlord," she says. "Maybe this year you can tie it down while I pat it fast with mud."

Somehow, as she smokes her stolen cigarette and I eat my popcorn, she makes the job of thatching the roof sound like a joy.

"With the money from this year's crop," she says, "we may have enough to make you a new dress. Perhaps from that red-and-gold fabric you've been eyeing at Bajai Sita's store."

I lower my eyes, embarrassed and glad all at once.

"Maybe," I say, "there will be enough to go to Bajai Sita and buy sugar for sweet cakes."

"Maybe," she says, "we can buy extra seed this year and plant the empty field behind the hut."

"Maybe," I say, "we can borrow Gita's uncle's water buffalo. I can drive the plow and you can spread the seed."

We sit there in the flickering light of a shallow saucer of oil, already rich with harvest money.

As we linger over the last of our luxuries—Ama inhales her cigarette down to a stub, I wipe a stubborn last kernel from the bowl with my fingertip—we don't say what we both know.

That the first thing we must do is pay the landlord.
And Gita's uncle, who sold us last season's seed.
And the headman's wife, who would not trade cooking oil
for work.
And my teacher, who gave me her own pencil when she saw
I had none.
And the owner of the tea shop, who, my stepfather says,
cheats at cards.

Instead, we linger over a luxury that costs nothing:
Imagining what may be.

WHAT THE MONSOON DOES

It doesn't rain constantly during the monsoon.

There is usually a shower in the morning that leaves behind stripes of color in the sky.

And another in the afternoon that leaves the rice plants plump and drowsy.

But all night, there is a long, soaking rain that leaves the footpaths sloppy and hearts refreshed.

TOO MUCH OF A GOOD THING

Eight days and nights and nothing but rain.
Curtains of rain that blind me, even on the short, familiar
path to the privy.

TRYING TO REMEMBER

The rain is so fierce, so relentless, so merciless, it finds every crack in our roof.

Ama and I pack the walls with scraps of cloth, but each day they melt a little more.

When there is a rare moment of sun, the women gather on the slope, shake their heads, and say this is the worst monsoon in years.

After several more days, when there is no sun at all, the village headmen gather in the tea shop and ask the holy man to say a special prayer to make it stop.

I wait at home, as the damp firewood sizzles and smokes, trying to keep the baby from catching a chill. He wrestles with the blanket, bored and cranky from days on end inside.

While I try to remember the days when the heat was so fierce, so relentless, so merciless, that we prayed for this rain.

WHAT DISASTER SOUNDS LIKE

When the night rain soaks the ground past the soaking point, when the earthen walls around the paddy melt away, when the rice plants are sucked out of the earth one by one and washed down the slope, there should be a sound, a noise announcing that something is terribly wrong.

Instead there is a ghostly hush that tells us we have lost everything.

A BITTER HARVEST

I tell Ama not to weep, that surely there are a few stalks of rice left in our field. I run outside and splash through what remains of our paddy. With frantic hands I claw at the mud.

Finally, when I stand, my hands aching with emptiness, I see Gita's family in the plot below ours. Gita's father did not spend his afternoons in the tea shop; he spent his days building paddy walls that could stand up to the monsoon. Now he faces the swallow-tailed peak, his hands in a prayer of gratitude. His rice plants bow to the sun, his little boy splashes in the mud.

My stomach churns with something bitter. I do not know if it is hunger.
Or envy.

THE PRICE OF A LOAN

My stepfather has been gone a week and a day. He said he was going to visit his brother two villages away to ask for a loan. But I wonder, when I see the owner of the tea shop looking at Ama with squinty coin eyes, if my stepfather has run away.

Ama has been gone since daybreak. She said she was going to the village to sell our hen and her chicks. But I wonder, when I picture Bajai Sita and her little lizard face, if Ama will get more than a pocketful of rice.

Ama and I can do without food, but the baby is beginning to grow listless. Now, as he whimpers in his basket, I wish for the noisy cries that I used to wish away.

I watch for Ama on the path below, and wonder what will be lost next.

Later, when I see her climbing the hill to our hut, I know.

It is the joyful noise of her earrings.
And the proud set of her head.

HOW LONG THIS WILL LAST

Although the path to our hut has washed away, a parade of people comes to the door.

First is the landlord.

He asks for my stepfather, but Ama says it is she who will pay the rent this time. She unwinds her waistcloth, removes a handful of rupee notes from her money pouch, and sends him on his way.

Then comes Gita's uncle. He looks at our paddy, our hut, then at the baby, and says he will take half of what we owe.

The headman's wife is next. She says full payment is due, as well as 50 rupees extra for interest.

I do not go to school, so I do not have to face my pretty, moonfaced teacher empty-handed.

We eat rice and lentils with the money Ama got for her earrings. The baby eats curds and fruit and grows fat and feisty again. One night, Ama makes sweet cakes with Bajai Sita's sugar. My stomach complains a bit, unaccustomed to such richness, but I don't let on to Ama, who watches me but does not eat.

We are, in the evenings as we sit by lamplight, happy.

I wonder, though, how long it will be before the owner of the tea shop knocks on our door.

Or how many nights until my stepfather comes home with another debt to repay.

Or, if he never returns, how long until the money in Ama's waistcloth runs out.

STRANGER

A strange man is climbing toward our hut. He is wearing a city coat and a triangle hat, high on one side and low on the other, like the one the landlord wears on rent day.

The women at the spring have talked of government men who hand out money to people who sign papers.

I will read the words for Ama and show her where to sign. Then we won't have to worry about anything.

Suddenly, though, I am afraid. I have never spoken to a city man. So I run inside and peek at him through the window.

Ama is bent over in the field. She straightens up, sees the man, and walks toward him. Then she kneels and touches her brow to his feet.

I see then that this stranger is my stepfather in a big-shoulders city coat and a hat that sits on his head like a lopsided mountain peak.

Ama stands and goes to the fire to bring him some lentils. She puts a finger to her lip as she goes past me.

"Even a man who gambles away what little we have on a fancy hat and a new coat," she says, "is better than no man at all."

FESTIVAL OF LIGHTS

On the first day of the festival, we honor the crows. We put out offerings of rice because crows are the messengers for the lord of death.

On the second day, we honor the dogs. We dot their foreheads with red powder and place marigold garlands around their necks because dogs are the guides to the land of the dead.

And on the third day, we clean our homes top to bottom. We put out dozens of tiny oil lamps at dusk to welcome the goddess Lakshmi, my namesake, who will circle the earth and bestow wealth and blessings on the humble and the pure.

Our family has no grain to spare for the crow and nothing for the stray dog, save a kick from my stepfather's sandal.

Still, Ama says we must prepare for Lakshmi's arrival. Ama sweeps every corner of our hut and sets the blankets out to air. Then she twists tiny bits of rag into wicks and places them in shallow clay saucers, each with a drop of oil.

When my chores are done, I sit out in the sun in front of our hut and string a necklace of marigolds. We have no dog, so I make the garland for Tali. But when I go to place the wreath over her head, she shrinks away. I scratch the place between her ears just the way she likes. Then, as her head droops with contentment, I slip the garland around her neck.

She sniffs and sneezes and shakes her head from side to side. Then she bends low, her ear to the ground, and tries to wriggle out of it. Finally, she gets to her feet, and with one grand, impatient toss of her head, she throws the garland in the dirt. And eats it.

Ama comes by and smiles. "That goat," she says. "Perhaps she is not so silly after all."

AN AUSPICIOUS NIGHT

A thousand stars have fallen to earth.

That, at least, is how it looks to me as I sit outside our hut and look down the mountainside at all the houses below, each windowsill and doorway adorned with tiny lanterns, lighting the way for the goddess Lakshmi.

"This is an auspicious night," says Ama. Her brisk and steady hand flies through my hair as she twines the strands into braids. "The goddess Lakshmi will see our lights and bring us good fortune."

My stepfather comes out of the hut, wearing his kingly hat and his big-shoulders coat. He pats his chest, and I see Ama's money pouch around his neck.

"This," he says, "is an auspicious night. This is the night when the goddess favors gamblers."

And because it is my favorite night of the year, the festival of my namesake, I let myself believe him.

AT THE FESTIVAL

Ama and I walk down to the village, my little brother riding on her back. As we draw near the bonfire, Ama presses a coin into my palm. "Run off and buy yourself a sweet cake," she says, "like the other children."

I tell her I'm not a child anymore. I tell her not to waste her money. But she insists.

"Tonight," she says, "you are a child."

POSSIBILITY

As I stand before the bonfire, licking the last of the sweet-
cake crumbs from my fingers, a city woman comes and
stands next to me. She is wearing a dress of yellow cloud
fabric, a hundred silver bangles on her wrists and ankles.
She smells of amber and night flowers.

"Where I live," she says, "the girls have sweet cakes every
day."

This delicate stranger, it seems, is speaking to me.
I steal a sideways look at her.

She smiles, drawing her shawl to her lips with the dignity of
a queen.

I, too, draw my shawl to my face, see that I have the callused
hands of a farm girl, and stuff them in the pockets of my
homespun skirt.

"City girls have pretty dresses," she says from behind her
yellow cloud. "And fancy baubles. They eat oranges, dates,
and mangoes every day. It is the easy life."

"You?" I say, my voice as tiny as a bug's. "You're a maid?"

The city woman laughs, still hiding her mouth with the hem
of her shawl, but she does not answer.

"Would you like to come to the city with me?" she says.
"I will be your auntie."

I nod yes-no-yes-no and run back to Ama, afraid to tell her
about this new auntie who smells of amber and jasmine
and possibility.

WINDFALL

We are awakened in the middle of the night by a thunderous roaring outside our hut. Ama and I come down to see my stepfather seated on a machine with two wheels and a pair of metal antlers.

"It is a motorcycle," he says. "I won it from a city boy home for the festival."

The metal beast coughs, and great blasts of smoke come from its tail.
"I told you this was an auspicious night," my stepfather says.

I do not see how this thing is of any use to us.
But Ama hugs me and whispers in my ear that we will trade the beast at Bajai Sita's. In an instant I see it all. We will buy back Ama's earrings. We will have enough money for a drum of cooking oil, a barrel of flour, a new dress for me and one for Ama, a jacket for the baby, a tin roof.

Perhaps, I think grudgingly, even enough for a new vest for my stepfather.

THE NEXT DAY

In the morning, my stepfather is up early, tending lovingly to
his beast.
He rubs it down with a rag and talks to it like a baby.

"We are going to the tea shop," he tells it, "so that everyone
can envy my good fortune."

The beast, however, balks at his suggestion. It belches and
breaks wind, but it will not roar the way it did last night.
My stepfather kicks the thing, curses at it, then finally it
snarls in reply. My stepfather rides away, slipping and sliding
in the mud.

NIGHTFALL

It is nearly dark when my stepfather comes back from the tea
shop.
The beast is nowhere to be seen, and my stepfather is on
foot, without his city coat or even his hat.

Ama runs to the door, sees, then turns her face to the corner
so as not to shame him when he comes in and climbs the
ladder to the sleeping loft.

A TINY EARTHQUAKE

Ama has to be coaxed from bed the next morning with a cup of hot tea. She says she is not ill, but she has the look of a great sickness about her.

I put the baby in a basket on my back and go about my chores, all the while keeping my eyes on Ama. Her steps are slow and heavy, and she stops often in her work to shake her head and sigh.

At noon, I warm the remains of yesterday's soup, feed it to the baby, then tighten my waistcloth so my own hungry stomach will think it is full. Then I go in search of Ama so that she can wipe the bowl clean with the last heel of bread. When she doesn't answer my calls, I go outside and find her hiding behind Tali's shed, weeping.

"What is it, Ama?" I say.

Ama wipes her cheek with the hem of her shawl. "Your stepfather has said you must go to the city and earn your keep as a maid."

This news is like a tiny earthquake, shaking the very ground beneath my feet. And yet, for Ama, I stand firm.

"This is good news, Ama," I say, my voice full of a boldness I did not know I had. "There will be one less mouth to feed here, and I will send my wages home."

Ama nods weakly.

"If I go, you will have money enough for rice and curds, milk and sugar. Enough for a coat for the baby and a sweater for you."

She smiles wanly and strokes my cheek with her work-worn hand.

"Enough," I say, "for a tin roof."

CITY RULES

In the city, says Ama, the people clean the floors with one rag and the dishes with another. Take care not to mix them up, or you will risk a beating.

Get up early in the morning before anyone else in the house and be the last one to bed at night. Never sit down in the presence of your mistress or her husband or even in front of the children. And never eat your meal until they have gone to bed. This will prove what a hard worker you are.

Hide your wages inside your blouse. That way, she says, you will fool anyone who thinks you keep your money in your waistcloth.

Do not eat any food that comes in a paper wrapper. You do not know who has cooked it.

Put a pinch of cardamom in the rice, she says. This will make it more filling.

Stay two steps behind your mistress if you are helping her with the marketing, and keep your head bowed when you are in public so that the city men cannot see your face.

Say your prayers every day and wash your skirt and blouse once a month.

"You will make us proud," Ama says, "as the first member of our family to leave the mountain. And perhaps at festival time next year, your mistress will let you come back to visit. Then you can tell us all about the world beyond this one."

A TRADE

The next morning my stepfather brings me to Bajai Sita's store. He is carrying Ama's empty firewood basket and yet he is wearing his vest, his watch, and his best trousers.

"Lakshmi wants to go to work in the city," he tells her.

I feel myself grow taller with his words.

Bajai Sita regards me through little lizard eyes. "Is she a hard worker?" she asks.

"She needs a thrashing on occasion," my stepfather says, "but she is not as lazy as some."

My cheeks flame with indignation, but I say nothing.

"Are you willing to do whatever is asked of you?" she says.

I nod.

I will use a separate rag to wash the dishes, I want to tell her, and I will wait to take my meal until night.

"Yes," I say. "I will do as I am told."

She goes behind a curtain and returns with the stranger in the yellow dress.

The woman looks me over head to toe, then addresses my

stepfather. "How much do you want for her?" she asks, her veil to her lips.

My stepfather squints. He takes in the costly fabric of the woman's dress, the baubles on her ears, the silver bangles on her wrist. "One thousand rupees," he says.

There are not that many rupees in the world! I cringe at his backwardness and pray this refined and lovely city woman does not laugh him out of the store.

Instead, she motions for him to step inside the back room with her. "She has no hips," I hear her say. "And she's plain as porridge. I'll give you five hundred."

I do not understand. I can carry a load of firewood so heavy it would put a man to shame, and my legs are sturdy enough to climb the mountain a dozen times in one day. What does it matter that I have no hips yet?

My stepfather says he knows the going rate for a young girl like me. "No less than eight hundred."

"I will give you half now and the rest when she has proved her worth," she says.

My stepfather grunts, and he and the woman return.

Bajai Sita unfurls a roll of rupee notes from her waistcloth.

My stepfather counts the money, then counts it again.

"Your family will get nothing, not one rupee, if you do not obey your new auntie," says Bajai Sita. "Do you understand?"

I don't. I don't understand at all. A great deal of money has just been paid for work I have not yet done. But I nod.

My stepfather counts the money one more time.

"Tell Ama I will make her proud," I say. "Tell her I'll be back for the next festival season."

But he has his eyes fixed on the wares on Bajai Sita's shelves. He is taking things and putting them in Ama's empty basket: a carton of cigarettes, a bag of sweets, chewing gum, a bottle of rice wine, and a new hat.

While he is busy haggling with Bajai Sita over a watch that has caught his eye, I place two things in the basket: a sweater for Ama and a coat for the baby.

It is a rich and happy day for our family, an 800-rupee day, a festive and auspicious day, and so I add one more thing for Ama: a costly treat that only the headman's wife can afford—a bottle of Coca-Cola, the sweet drink that people say is like having tiny fireworks in your mouth.

My stepfather scowls, but he does not say anything. On any other day, he would not tolerate such defiance, especially from a mere girl.

But today, I am no mere girl.

A SECOND LOOK

As Auntie and I leave the store, I see Krishna coming down the dirt road with his flock of goats. He is whistling and coaxing a straggler to join the others by tickling its rump with a long stem of elephant grass.

I pray that he will look in my direction, but, as always, his eyes are fixed on the ground before him. I want to tell him where I'm going, to tell him I that I will return as soon as I am able with a cash dowry for our wedding. I want to tell him to wait for me.

"Eyes forward," Auntie says. "No sense looking back."

I lower my head and obey.

But as we reach the end of the village, I turn around one last time. And steal one last look at the boy I have been watching for as long as I can remember.

MOVING FORWARD

Auntie says I must walk ahead of her even though I do not know the way.

"I will be behind you," she says.

I am too shy to tell her I won't run off, too timid to tell her how proud and nervous and excited I am to be the first person in my family to leave the mountain.

I feel a tiny sting on the backs of my legs, and I realize that Auntie has thrown a handful of gravel at my heels. To keep me moving forward.

A NEW WORLD

We have been walking all day. We have traveled through three villages, where the people pause in their labors and gape at us, and where even the water buffalo stare at us with the solemn eyes of old men.

I stare, too, at all the things I've never seen before.
A man pulling a wild boar on a rope.
A herd of yak hauling sacks of salt.
A mail runner ringing a cluster of bells as he nears a village.
A rope footbridge strung like a spiderweb.
A river that runs white.
And a man with teeth entirely of gold.

I ask Auntie how she knows the way to the city. She says that we are simply following the footsteps of all the others who have gone before us.

I try to remember each hut, each village. I try to memorize each twist in the path so I can find my way home at festival time next year. But when I close my eyes, each hut, each village, each twist in the road looks the same. And when I open my eyes and look behind us, the poinsettias stir in the wind, as if touched by fire.

It is a new world.
But there is one constant:

the mighty swallow-tailed peak.
It grows smaller the farther we walk,
but still, it is always there, waiting to guide me back.

WHAT I CARRY

Inside the bundle Ama packed for me are:
my bowl,
my hairbrush,
the notebook my teacher gave me for being the number one
girl in school,
and my bedroll.

Inside my head I carry:
my baby goat,
my baby brother,
my ama's face,
our family's future.

My bundle is light.
My burden is heavy.

QUESTIONS AND ANSWERS

Auntie and I have been walking for two days and a half. We have passed through seven villages, each one invisible to the other because of the mountain between them, but each one the same, with women pounding laundry on rocks at the village fountains and men sitting cross-legged in the tea shops.

We go up and down hills, sometimes following a dirt path, sometimes following an empty riverbed. Sometimes following no trail at all.

When we stop to rest, Auntie pulls a packet of betel leaf tobacco from her waistcloth. She stuffs a wad of it between her gum and teeth, rocks back on her heels, and chews.

"Auntie," I say finally. "Tell me about the city."

She spits, and a stream of red betel juice lands on the ground between us.
"You will have to see it for yourself."

"Is it true that all the roofs are covered in gold?"

"Where did you hear that?" she says.

"In school." I want Auntie to know that I am not a backward girl. I am educated.

She spits again and says that I am very smart, that I will do well in the city.

I have a hundred questions:
How long will it take for us to get there?
How do I address my mistress?
How can I find Gita?

But I ask only one:
"What are these things called movies?"

Auntie says that in the city, people gather and pay money to see beautiful women and handsome men put on a show. The people in the show are called movie stars.

"Are you a movie star, Auntie?"

She smiles, and I see then what was behind the shawl she always draws to her lips: a mouth of blackened teeth.

I smile back, but inside I am a tiny bit afraid of my new auntie.

AN INAUSPICIOUS START

At the ninth village, Auntie tells me we will ride the rest of the way. My feet silently thank her while I sit by the side of the road and wait for a bullock cart to appear.

She points to a metal wagon with two men inside and says I am to sit in the back, in the open, along with the cucumbers and chickens. I climb up, my bundle at my side, while Auntie gets in front. Suddenly, the beast roars, a hundred times louder than my stepfather's motorcycle, and I cry out in terror.

The cart lunges forward. All at once we are moving fast over the dirt road as the huts-and-shops-and-huts-and-shops rush by in a blur.

I squawk just like the chickens, clap a hand over my mouth to try to stop myself, and cry out again as this roaring, lurching cart jounces and bounces in and out of every rut in the road, until finally I am laughing at the sheer madness of it.

Soon, though, I can feel my breakfast of tea and rice water coming up my throat. I clamp my teeth together. But the bitter meal surges up onto my tongue and flies out of my mouth without warning.

I wipe my mouth. Soon I am smiling again. Because, as I bounce along back here, only the chickens know about this inauspicious start to my journey.

THE CITY

We have been bumping along a dirt road for hours when our cart is joined by another, then another, then another. Some have people sitting inside them. Some have people riding on top. Some have animals inside. Some have animals on top. Some carts bleat like goats. Some whine like mosquitoes. Some have two wheels, some have three, some have too many to count. Soon the road is all madness and noise.

This must be the city.

NEXT

As our cart shoulders its way along the road,
I crane my neck this way,
then that,
looking at
a man scooping hot popcorn into a paper cone, next to
a barber lathering an old man's face, next to
a boy plucking the feathers from a lifeless chicken, next to
an ear cleaner, his customer grunting with satisfaction, next to
a woman whose arms are draped with a hundred necklaces, next to
a man with a flute, coaxing a snake out of a basket, next to
a tailor pumping the treadles of his sewing machine, next to
a bone seller rattling his wares, next to
a woman with a basket heaped with dates, next to
a pig nosing through a pile of trash, next to
a boy ladling oil out of a tin, next to
a man selling broken pieces of motorcycles, next to
a girl threading marigolds on a string, next to
a man with crates of pigeons for sale, next to
a woman serving tea, next to
a boy shining shoes, next to
a water buffalo napping in the shade, next to
a man selling cucumbers, next to
a man chanting a prayer, next to
a man scooping hot popcorn into a paper cone.

And I wonder,

In this swarming, hurry-up city,

what will happen

next

to me.

ON THE BUS

The cart we're riding on now is called a bus. I don't know this for certain, but I am fairly sure that that is its name because Auntie said, "Don't pester me with a thousand questions when we get on the bus."

Here is what I know so far:
The carts with chicken and sheep in the back are called trucks.
The ones with people inside are cars.
A fire inside makes them go.
People here live in solid-wall huts that are stacked on top of each other.
City people are not angry at each other; they don't greet one another because they don't know each other.

The bus has soft benches and it holds a village full of people. It smells of onions and curry and cigarette smoke, and a baby who has soiled his cloth, and other things I cannot name.

The man next to me empties his nose out the window, pinching one side shut and blowing on the other, and for a moment I am afraid that I will lose my meal again.

Auntie is asleep, her head drooping heavily on my shoulder.
I don't move.

I look out the window.

A man with a table strapped to his back is walking down the middle of the road. The bus bleats, and the man scuttles out of the way like a lizard darting into its hole. A cow is sleeping in the middle of the road. The bus goes around her.

Another bus with another village full of people comes straight toward us, then slips off to our side and passes by in a rush of wind.

At first I nearly cry out. But then I look around at stone faces of the city people and understand that that is not done here.

I study the scene in front of the bus the way I studied my letters in school. Gradually I begin to make out a kind of order in all the disorderliness, a pattern to it all. It is like a river, where the currents of buses and trucks and people and animals flow into and around each other. If you look hard enough, chaos turns into order the way letters turn into words.

This city is not so hard. You just have to study it.
Auntie is right. I'll do well here.

SEEING A GIRL WITH A LONG BLACK BRAID

There are a thousand girls in the city.
But so far, none of them is Gita.

LOST

I do not understand.

The bus has left the city.

And we are traveling on a hard black road.

Everyone on the bus is asleep.

No matter which way I turn,

I cannot see the swallow-tailed peak.

MORE QUESTIONS

When the sun comes up, the people on the bus begin to stir.
A man with a rooster in a metal basket throws a cloth over it,
but the old bird cannot be fooled; he announces the new
day insistently.

When Auntie wakes up, I ask her why we are no longer in
the city.
She tells me not to worry.
"That was just a small city," she says. "We are going to a much
bigger city, a grand city, a city by the water."

I take some comfort in her words. This explains why the
roofs in the first city were not covered in gold.
But I am also worried. If there are *two* cities, which one is
Gita in?

NEW CLOTHES

We have driven through a half-dozen cities and have arrived at a strange, solid-wall hut with many rooms. The family here seems to have many amas, a few men, but no children.

Auntie takes me into one of the rooms. There is nothing in it but a stained straw mat. "Take off those filthy hill clothes," she says.

It is immodest to undress in the presence of another, and so I wait for Auntie to leave. But she clucks her tongue like an angry hen and tells me I will have to get over my backward country ways. Then she holds out a pink dress of cloud fabric and a pair of shoes.

"For me?" I say.

She clucks again and says we haven't got all day.

I walk to the corner, turn my back to her, wriggle out of my own clothes, then lift the soft pink petticoat over my head. The new dress seems to be one long piece of cloth, with no beginning and no end, material so light and fine, I feel more naked than dressed inside it.

Auntie turns me to face her. I cover myself with my hands, but Auntie pries them away, saying I am a hopeless rube. She wraps the fabric once around my waist, then once more, twists and tucks it in at my hip. I cannot imagine how I will walk freely in such a long, flowing gown, or how I will be able to haul the firewood and scrub the floors in such a fine and flimsy dress.

Auntie points to the shoes. "These go on your feet," she says.

I want her to know that I know about shoes, that I had a pair of sandals when my father was alive. But my feet, bare and tough and dirty from three days of travel, would make my words seem like lies. So I put the shoes on as if I do so every day.

Instantly, my feet howl. These shoes are nothing but tight little boxes. I clench my toes, like a bat grasping a branch, as I stuff my old homespun clothes into my bundle and try to keep up with Auntie as she hurries from the room.

NUMBERS

Auntie is speaking to a man in a tongue I do not understand. Some of the words are familiar, but most of them rush by like the huts-and-shops-and-huts-and-shops, making my head hurt from the speed of this city talk.

It seems as though they are talking about me now. The man, who has a nose like a turnip, points to me and asks Auntie a question. The answer, as best I can tell, is the number twelve.

He trains his eyes on me and my pink dress, and I imagine that he can see right through it. I wrap my arms around myself.

"How old are you?" he says in my language.

I tell him I am thirteen.

He wheels around and slaps Auntie across the face, and she turns from a woman of queenly bearing to a frightened child.

The turnip-nose man lets out a stream of angry words I cannot follow, but I understand that I have done wrong. I fall to my knees and beg the man to forgive me.

But he and Auntie are laughing. They are speaking in a strange language, but it seems that they are trading numbers.

Auntie names a price as high as a mountain.

The man spits.

Auntie names another figure.

The turnip-nose man answers with a smaller amount.

Auntie goes high.

The man goes low.

Eventually they agree and the man gives Auntie a roll of rupee notes.

I do not know what they have agreed to.

But I do know this:

he gives her nearly enough money to buy a water buffalo.

UNCLE HUSBAND

Auntie has gone, leaving me in the room with the turnip-nose man. I have never been alone with a man who is not in my family. I pull my shawl over my head and hide inside the pink cloud fabric. But the man comes close, so close I can smell the sour stink of his hair oil.

He smiles, reaches in his pocket and offers me a sweet. I do not want to cross this slapping man, so I take it.

"When will Auntie return?" I ask.

"Bimla?" the man says.

I do not know her proper name. I only know her as Auntie. I shrug yes-no-I-don't-know.

"Don't worry," he says. "You will see your Auntie Bimla again after we cross the border."

I don't know this word, border, but I have learned from Auntie that city people don't like to be asked a lot of questions.

"From now on," he says, "I will be your uncle. But you must call me husband. Do you understand?"

I don't. Not at all. But I nod.

"The border is a very dangerous place," he says. "There are

bad men there, men with guns, men who might harm you, or try to take you away from me and Auntie."

It is all so confusing. I am afraid of this man. But I also feel grateful that he will protect me from the bad border men with guns.

"Don't be frightened," he says kindly. "It is a pretend game. You like games, don't you?"

I nod.

Gita and I used to play pretend games. When we played make-believe, I sometimes had a husband. But it was Krishna, the young goatherd with sleepy cat eyes, not an old, turnip-nose man who doles out sweets and slaps with the same hand.

CROSSING THE BORDER

The cart we are traveling in now is called a rickshaw. It is pulled by a chicken-legged man in a rag skirt. Uncle Husband and I sit on a seat in the back, while all around us are carts of every kind, spewing smoke and churning dust.

Our rickshaw sits in a long line of trucks and cars going nowhere while people on foot pass by. One of those people is Auntie. I place my palms together to greet her, then I remember the city lesson I have learned, and let my hands fall back in my lap as I watch her thread her way through the crowd.

Uncle Husband leans close and slips a sweet into my palm. "You like sweets, don't you?" he says.

During the hungry months I have eaten porridge thickened with dirt, rotten potatoes, boiled weeds. I nod. I like sweets. I like them more than I can say.

I nod and then remember to whisper thank you.

Up ahead, I see one of the bad border men. He is dressed all in tan and he has a gun at his hip. He stops each cart and asks questions.

Uncle Husband puts an arm around my shoulder. "Don't be afraid," he says. "I will take care of you."

The border man steps up to our cart. He and Uncle Husband speak in quick city talk, examining an important-looking piece of paper that Uncle Husband has taken from his vest.

The border man points to the paper and asks me, "Is this your husband?"

I curl my toes inside my new shoes and say yes.

The man places a hand on his hip, and I wait for him to shoot me for this lie. But he simply walks on to the next cart.

Soon we are moving, the feet of the rickshaw puller padding noiselessly on the dirt path. I ask Uncle Husband when we will cross the border. He says we already have.

A REWARD

Uncle says I have done well, and he gives me a handful of sweets. I eat one and stow the others in my bundle.

He yells at the chicken-legged man, cursing at him and telling him to go faster.

Next time Uncle is in a good mood, I will ask him where I can find a mail runner to take the rest of the sweets back home to Ama.

TRAIN

Now we are riding on a train. It makes thunder when it moves, but somehow it rocks the people inside to sleep.

Uncle takes a flat pouch from his vest, puffs his cheeks out, and blows into it.
The thing fills slowly with his breath, and soon it takes the shape of a giant lentil bean.
Then he puts it behind his head and closes his eyes.

When he wakes up I will ask him when we will see Auntie again.

In the meantime, I am writing in my notebook about the strange things I have seen so far: all the houses here have glass suns like the one in Gita's hut. And the men carry devices that trill like birds and cause them to shout *Hello! Hello!* And everywhere I look, there are pictures of beautiful, full-hipped women and handsome men with glossy hair. I am not sure, but I think they must be movie stars.

Since we crossed the border, everything is different, even the language on the signs.

"We are in India now," Uncle Husband has told me. "Don't speak to anyone here. If they hear you talk, they will know you're from the mountains and they will try to take advantage of you."

But while he's sleeping, I write a few of these India words in my notebook. Maybe, if my wealthy mistress is pleased with my work, she will teach me what they mean.

When I have run out of words to copy, I look out the window at this strange place called India. Inside the train, the people around me are snoring. I don't understand how they can close their eyes when there is so much to see.

ONE HUNDRED ROTIS

The train has stopped at a giant metal hut. Through the window, I can see a man with a grill stacked with a hundred rotis.

People run from the train and line up at his cart. His mountain of bread begins to disappear.

My stomach churns, looking at so much food vanishing so fast.

Uncle Husband tells me to stay in my seat. Then he joins the line of people at the cart. Soon he comes back to the train with a steaming roti, fragrant with home and Ama.

I go weak with wanting.

"For you," he says.

I go weak with gratitude.

Uncle Husband isn't young and handsome like Krishna, and I can never tell when he might grow angry and slap me. But I am grateful, in this strange new world of moving thunder and invisible borders, that he is my Uncle Husband.

CITY WAYS

The train slows to a halt. Uncle Husband tells me to stand up, that we are making a stop. I don't understand. Still, I am glad of the chance to get out of this traveling oven and move my legs.

We leave the train, and I see that the men are going to one side, women to another. Uncle Husband puts a hand to my cheek. His touch is soft. His words are hard.

"Come right back. Don't try anything. Or your family will not see a single rupee."

I swallow, nod, and join the river of women flowing into a field beside the train.

Then, all around me, the women lift their skirts, squat like crows, and relieve themselves on the open ground. I feel shame for them, doing in front of others what is rightly done in private. And I am almost ill, as the odor of so much waste swirls around me. But my own need for relief is so strong, I have no choice but to do as they do.

I copy their crow pose, but somehow I wet a corner of my long flowing dress.
Now my shame is for myself.

DISGRACED

As I walk back to the train, I pass a cluster of men yelling and shaking their fists in the air. At the center of the group, a girl my age crouches in the dirt. Her scalp has been freshly shaved—pale and fragile as a bird's egg—and hanks of her long dark hair lie in coils at her feet.

One of the men in the crowd throws his cigarette butt at her feet. Another one spits in her direction. Then another—a fat old man with a boil on his neck—picks up a handful of gravel and flings it at her. She winces, then begins to cry.

I see Uncle Husband standing at the edge of the circle, puffing on a cigarette, taking in the scene with untroubled eyes. I run over to his side.

"What is happening?" I ask. "What did she do to deserve this kind of punishment?"

He grinds his cigarette out with his boot and sighs. "That's what she gets," he says, "for trying to run away from her husband."

He points to the old man with the boil on his neck.

The old husband's cheeks are flushed with pride now as he grabs the girl by the arm and leads her away. She is squirming and crying, dragging her feet in the dirt.

"Stupid girl," says Uncle Husband.

I don't understand.

"One look at that head of hers and anyone can tell she's a disgraced woman," he says.
"Even if she does run off again, no one will help her."

A CITY OF THE DEAD

The sun is not yet up when Uncle Husband tells me that we've reached our destination. As the train glides to a stop, I hold my bundle close and look out the window for the golden roofs.

What I see first is one hut,
swaybacked as an old water buffalo.
Then another,
and another,
until there is nothing but hut after hut
after hut
after hut.

There are roofs made of metal scraps,
held down with the soft black wheels from cars.
There are roofs of heavy paper,
piled with bricks and boots and pots and pans.
And roofs made of sheets
tied in place with plastic vines.

But no roofs of gold.
No date or mango or orange trees.
And no movie stars.

Only rows of sleeping bodies. Side by side by side are men, women, and children in rags, asleep on the ground.

I try to count them,
get to two hundred
and give up
when I see two hundred more beyond them.

Uncle Husband says to stay close as we get off the train. Outside, the air is warm and heavy, thick with the smoke of a hundred cooking fires. The sky is so choked with dust that the light from the electric suns on poles disappears in the haze. All around us, people shuffle along, heads down, eyes empty, as the dust churns at their feet.

I am afraid of this city where the lying-down people look like the dead. And the standing-up ones, like the walking dead.

WALKING IN THE CITY

It is hard to walk in my new shoes, harder still to push through streets jammed with scrawny rickshaw men hauling plump passengers, naked children pawing through rubbish heaps, stray dogs nosing through gutters filled with human waste.

At one street corner, two boys are begging for coins. One has a leg that ends in a stump where his knee should be. He cups his hand and brings it to his mouth as if he is eating invisible food.

The other has a music-making machine. He wears one glove and does a dance that makes it look as if he's walking even though he's not going anywhere.

The people drop their coins in the dancing boy's cup, avoiding the hungry eyes of the other one.

A man in baggy trousers twists the tail of his water buffalo to make him go faster. Uncle Husband presses his fist into my back to make me go faster.

HAPPINESS HOUSE

Finally, we turn down an alley and arrive in front of a metal gate held fast with a heavy chain. Uncle takes a key from his vest, opens the lock, and hurries me inside.

"Will Auntie be here?" I say.

"Who?" He is distracted, locking the chain behind us.

"Auntie Bimla," I say. "Will she be here?"

"Later," he says. "She'll be here later."

Beyond the gate, a man lies sleeping in front of a door. Uncle nudges him with the toe of his boot. The man rises, lets us in, then locks the door behind us.

This place is dark as a cave, and it smells of liquor and incense.

As my eyes adjust, I see a dozen sleeping girls, some in the corners, some on rope cots.

"What kind of place is this?" I ask uncle.

"Happiness House," he says. "Auntie Mumtaz will explain it all to you."

In the weak morning light, I see that the girls are wearing dresses of every color. They have heavy silver bangles on

their wrists and ankles, and earrings of gold and jewels.
Their eyes are painted with black crayon, and their lips are
drawn on like red chilis.

At home, these girls would be up at dawn to do their chores,
not sleeping in their festival clothes until the midday meal.

I wonder if perhaps this Happiness House is where the
movie stars live.

TEN THOUSAND RUPEES

A figure rises from the corner and steps toward us. She has the reed-thin body of a girl and the hollow cheeks of an old woman. She is, under the folds of her yellow dress, frail as a baby bird.

Uncle speaks with her in brisk city language, and the aging bird girl disappears behind a curtain.

Moments later the cloth is drawn back. Inside a darkened chamber, a fat woman in a purple sari lounges on a cot. She has folds of flesh like roti dough at her waist, and a face as plump as an overripe mango.

She snaps her fingers and the bird girl flinches. Even Uncle Husband seems to draw back. He pushes me toward the fat mango woman, so close that I can see the bloom of hair on her upper lip.

I stand upright, so she can see what a strong worker I am.

She surveys me head to toe, then spits.

"How much?" she says to Uncle Husband.

"Fifteen thousand," he says.

The woman laughs. "For this one? She is thin as yesterday's tea."

They bargain back and forth, sometimes in my language, sometimes in another tongue. Uncle goes high, the woman goes low.

Eventually Uncle shrugs and gives up. The woman takes a record book out from inside the folds of her dress. She writes down the number 10,000.

The woman snaps her fingers, and the bird girl rises and takes me by the arm.
I look to Uncle Husband.

"Go on," he says impatiently. "She will find you a bed."

I am afraid to leave Uncle Husband, who protected me from the bad border men and bought me a roti, and who is the only person I know in this strange dead city. But I obey, pulling my bundle to my chest and following the girl down a hallway.

She takes me upstairs to a tiny room, unlocks the door, and gestures for me to enter.

"My Auntie Bimla is coming for me," I tell her.
"When she comes to the door, will you tell her I am here?"

I cannot tell if the girl understands. She doesn't answer.

She simply closes the door.

I don't know why I am in this strange house or where Auntie Bimla is. It seems as though this Auntie Mumtaz is my new mistress. She is a strict one, to be sure, but I will prove myself to her. And then my mother will have a new dress, shoes for the cold season, even a new shawl made of the finest yarn. My little brother will have fruit and curds twice a day and a jacket of yak fur. Even my stepfather can get new spectacles and a vest, I suppose. And our roof, our new tin roof, will be the shiniest one on the mountainside.

This is what I am thinking as I hear the girl lock the door behind her.

IN THIS ROOM

There are posters of gods and movie stars on the walls.
An electric sun hanging from the middle of the ceiling.
A rope bed.
A palm frond machine that stirs the air.
And iron bars on the windows.

A corner of the room is curtained off with a length of cloth
from an old sari.
On the floor, a plastic bucket sits next to a hole in the floor.
I can tell from the stink that this is the privy.

I sit on the bed and try to picture Tali's little pink nose.
The mists dancing around the swallow-tailed peak.
The tawny grain fields.
Ama's crow-black hair.
Krishna's sleepy cat eyes.

But my thoughts spin like the palm frond machine.

I think of the aging bird girl and wonder why she is so skinny
if she eats sweet cakes and dates and oranges and mangoes
every day.

I think of the woman with the rolls of roti dough at her waist
and wonder why she lives in this darkened cave building if
she is so rich.

And if she will teach me city words when I am finished with my chores.

But finally my eyes grow heavy and I lie down on the bed.
And after four days of traveling, I fall asleep.

HOMESICK

I awake for a moment, unsure of where I am.
I yawn and wait for the scent of hearth smoke and baking bread.
And what greets my nose is the stench of the privy hole next to my bed.
I pray for a mountain breeze, brisk with the promise of snow, and instead I see the palm frond machine lazily churning the same sultry city air.
I listen for the clucking of the hens.
What I hear are the fighting voices of a man and woman in the room next to mine.

So far, this city is not what I had hoped.

Perhaps if I close my eyes and fall asleep again,
I can at least dream of home.

TV

I awake when two girls come and unlock the door. One is pretty, with teardrop eyes and deep brown skin, like the hide of a nut. The other has a crooked face. Her right cheek is sunken, and the corner of her mouth is tugged down in a permanent half frown.

They take me to a room where the other girls have gathered.
The aging bird girl is there, as well as others.
Young ones dressed to look old, and old ones dressed to look young.
A naked baby sleeps on a blanket on the floor,
and a little girl in pigtails kneels at her mother's feet as she checks her scalp for lice.

There is no chatter or laughter like there is when the village women gather.
Instead they are all entranced by a black box with a large glass window in front.
Inside the box, a tiny woman is singing. She is wearing gold pants, and her hair is blowing in the wind.

The half-frowning girl pushes a button and the woman is gone.
A man sits at a table reading from a paper.
She pushes the button again and again,
and the picture inside the box changes again and again.

There is a woman scrubbing a pot, shaking her head.
Then there is a man hitting a ball with a paddle.
Then a schoolgirl drinking Coca-Cola.
Then back to the woman in the gold pants.

A man with slicked-back hair whispers in the woman's ear.
She puts a finger to his lips, then dances to the corner of the box and disappears.

I put my hand to my mouth and wait to see what will happen next.
The girl with the nut-brown skin leans toward me.
"It's a television," she says in my language. "TV."

I have heard about television. My stepfather says his brother received one as a dowry when his son married a wealthy girl.

There are no golden roofs here, but perhaps this city is a grand one after all—if every house has a TV.

A CITY GIRL

The fat woman in the purple sari walks into the room. The girl with the crooked face jumps up and turns off the TV. The dark-skinned girl sits and waits, while the others saunter away.

The fat woman asks angry questions in the city language.
"Yes, Mumtaz," says the dark-skinned girl.
"No, Mumtaz," says the frowning girl.

This Mumtaz pinches the skin above my elbow and twists it until my eyes sting.
I don't move. I don't say a word. Even when she lets go and shoves me toward the other girls.

Then Mumtaz is gone. And the dark-skinned girl is washing my face, the half-frowning one brushing my hair.

They do not speak, and I feel shy around these bold city girls, as they do for me what only my ama has done before.

"What are you doing?" I say.

The dark-skinned girl starts to answer, but the frowning one tells her to shush, and yanks the brush through my hair. She opens a tin box and removes a small bottle of red liquid. Then she takes my hand and paints the liquid on my nails, while the other girl uses a black crayon and draws on my eyelids.

"What is happening?" I say.

They don't answer.

The dark girl, the one who explained to me about the TV, says "Shhh." Then, when the frowning girl turns away, she whispers in my language, "You'll know soon enough."

I see my face reflected in a silver glass on the wall. Another Lakshmi looks back at me. She has black-rimmed tiger eyes, a mouth red as a pomegranate, and flowing hair like the tiny gold-pants woman in the TV.

She is fancy, like Auntie Bimla, like a movie star, like these other city girls.
I smile at this new Lakshmi. And she smiles back. Uncertainly.

OLD MAN

Mumtaz studies me.

"Are you ready to go to work?" she says in my language.

I nod and say yes, then nod again, although I do not understand how these city people do their chores in such fine clothes and uncomfortable shoes.

I follow Mumtaz down a hallway lined with tiny rooms. We pass by girls sitting cross-legged on the floor. Girls drawing on tiger eyes. Girls spraying themselves with flower water. Some of them stare at me. Some take no notice.

We go up some stairs, down another hallway, then into a room where an old man is lying on a bed. His skin is yellow and he has tufts of hair poking out from his ears. Mumtaz speaks kindly to him and I wonder if he is sick.

Across the hall, in another room, where a red cloth is hung across the doorway, I hear the sound of grunting. It is a strange, animal sound that makes me shudder.

Mumtaz points to me and says something to the old man. He licks his palm and smoothes down his hair. They do not seem to notice the grunting.

Then it stops. The red cloth is pulled back. And a man stands in the hallway zipping his pants.

I look down at my red-painted nails and my new shoes. Something is not right here. I don't know what is going on, but it is not right, not right at all.

Mumtaz pats the edge of the bed and tells me to come closer. The old man makes a clucking sound.

"Don't be afraid," she says. "Come here, now."

I don't move.

Her voice turns hard. "Get over here, you ignorant girl," she says.

Still, I do not move.

Then Mumtaz flies at me. She grabs me by the hair and drags me across the room. She flings me onto the bed next to the old man. And then he is on top of me, holding me down with the strength of ten men. He kisses me with lips that are slack and wet and taste of onions. His teeth dig into my lower lip.

Underneath the weight of him, I cannot see or move or breathe. He fumbles with his pants, forces my legs apart, and I can feel him pushing himself between my thighs. I gasp for air and kick and squirm. He thrusts his tongue in my mouth.

And I bite down with all my might.

He cries out "Aghh!" and I am running. Running down the hall, past the other girls, losing my fancy city shoes along the way, until I am back in the room where I started, pulling my old clothes out of my bundle.

SOLD

I'm wiping the makeup off my face when the dark-skinned girl comes in.
"What do you think you're doing?" she says.

"I'm going home."

Her tear-shaped eyes grow dark.

"There is a mistake," I tell her. "I'm here to work as a maid for a rich lady."

"Is that what you were told?"

Then Mumtaz arrives at the door, huffing, her mango face pink with anger.

"What do you think you're doing?" she says.

"Leaving," I say. "I'm going home."

Mumtaz laughs. "Home?" she says. "And how would you get there?"

I don't know.

"Do you know the way home?" she says.
"Do you have money for the train?
Do you speak the language here?
Do you even have any idea where you are?"

My heart is pounding like the drumming of a monsoon rain,
and my shoulders are shaking as if I had a great chill.

"You ignorant hill girl," she says.
"You don't know anything. Do you?"

I wrap my arms around myself and grip with all my might.
But the trembling will not stop.

"Well, then," Mumtaz says, pulling her record book out from
her waistcloth.
"Let me explain it to you."

"You belong to me," she says. "And I paid a pretty sum for
you, too."
She opens to a page in her book and points to the notation
for 10,000 rupees.

"You will take men to your room," she says. "And do whatever
they ask of you. You will work here, like the other girls, until
your debt is paid off."

My head is spinning now, but I see only one thing: the number
in her book. It warps and blurs, then fractures into bits that
swim before my eyes. I fight back tears and find my voice.

"But Auntie Bimla said—"

"Your 'auntie,' " she scoffs, "works for me."

I understand it all now.

I blink back the tears in my eyes. I ball my hands into fists. I will not do this dirty business. I will wait until dark and escape from Mumtaz and her Happiness House.

"Shahanna!" Mumtaz snaps her fingers and the dark-skinned girl hands her a pair of scissors.

This Shahanna leans close and whispers to me, "It will go easier on you if you hold still."

There is a slicing sound, and a clump of my hair falls to the floor. I cry out and try to break free, but Shahanna has hold of me.

Mumtaz draws back, the jaw of the scissors poised at my neck.
"Hold still," she says, her teeth clenched. "Or I'll slice your throat."

I look at Shahanna. Her eyes are wide with fear.

I stay very still, looking at the girl in the silver glass. Soon she has the shorn head of a disgraced woman and a face of stone.

"Try to escape with that head of hair," Mumtaz says, "and they'll bring you right back here."

And then they are gone, leaving me alone in the locked-in room.

I pound on the door.
I howl like an animal.
I pray.
I pace the room.
I kick the door.

But I do not cry.

THREE DAYS AND THREE NIGHTS

Each day, a thousand people pass below my window. Children on their way to school. Mothers hurrying home from the market. Rickshaw pullers, vegetable sellers, street sweepers and alms-seekers.

Not one looks up.

Each morning and evening Mumtaz comes, beats me with a leather strap, and locks the door behind her.

And each night, I dream that Ama and I are sitting outside our hut, looking down the mountain at the festival lights, and she is twining my hair into long dark braids.

WHAT'S LEFT

Tonight when Mumtaz comes to my room, she sees that her strap has left raw sores on my back and neck, my arms and legs.

So she hits me on the soles of my feet.

HUNGER

Tonight when Mumtaz comes and unlocks the door, she sees there is no part of me unmarked by her strap.

"Now will you agree to be with men?"

I shake my head.

And so she says that she will starve me until I submit.

What she does not realize is that I already know hunger.

I know how your stomach gnaws on itself searching for something to fill it.
I know how your insides keep moving, unwilling to believe they're empty.

I also know how to swallow your spit and pretend that it is soup.
How to close your nose to the scent of another family's supper fire.
And how to tie your waistcloth so tight that, at least for a few hours, you can fool your belly into thinking it's full.

Mumtaz, with her doughy waist and fat mango face,
doesn't know the match she's met in me.

WHAT I DON'T DO

I don't pay attention to cries of the peanut vendor under my window.

I don't let myself smell the onions frying in the kitchen below,
or pay heed to the chatter of the girls as they head past my door to the midday meal.

I don't listen for the footsteps of the street boy who brings afternoon tea in a wire caddy.

I don't permit myself to smell the aroma of the bowl of curried rice that Mumtaz passes under my nose, or take notice of the churning of my stomach.

Even in my sleep, I don't allow myself to dream of even a single roti.

AFTER FIVE DAYS

After five days of no food and water I don't even dream.

A CUP OF TEA

I have grown to dread one sound more than any other: the rasping of the key in the lock, which means that Mumtaz has arrived with her strap and her taunts.

And so I am in the corner of the locked-in room, my face to the wall, when the door opens. It is Shahanna, the girl with the nut-brown skin, holding a cup of tea.

She guides the cup to my mouth and talks softly.
"Take it," she says. "Your lips are cracked."

I sip, unwilling at first to let on how badly I want it, then I gulp it down greedily.

"Slow down," she says, gently prying the cup from my hand.
"If you go too fast, you will retch."

I do as she says, but soon, too soon, the cup is empty.

Shahanna reaches out and runs a gentle hand over my head.
"Your hair is already starting to grow back," she says.

I try to speak, but there is no voice in my throat after all these days with no one to talk to.
I want to tell this kind, dark-skinned girl about all the things I don't do.
That I don't think about my parched lips or my shorn hair.

That I don't look in the mirror.

But the words won't come.

"Mumtaz will let you live," she says, "if you do as she says."

I turn my back to her and look out the window.

Two schoolgirls in crisp blue uniforms skip by on the street below, holding hands.

"I've been out there," Shahanna says. "And I can tell you that it's not so bad here."

I am wary, knowing now how these city people cannot be believed.

"It's true," she says. "Out there, you're no better than a dog."

She points to a mongrel that has stopped to nose through a ditch full of human waste.

"Here at least we have a bed and food and clothes." She pauses.

I shake my head.

"No," I hear myself say in a ragged voice. "I will not do this disgraceful thing."

Shahanna sighs.

"She will only sell you to another place just like this."

She moves toward the door.

Inside I am begging her not to go, not to leave me alone watching the world go by outside my locked-in room. But on the outside I am blank. I have already learned from these city people. From the ones who turned a blind eye to the legless beggar boy, from the ones who shuffle through this city of the dead with their eyes empty.

You are safe here only if you do not show how frightened you are.

AFTER SHAHANNA'S VISIT

No one comes to my room. And I wonder if a day and night have passed, or two days and nights. Or a dozen days and nights.

A PRONOUNCEMENT

One day Mumtaz comes to my door without her strap.

"I have decided to let you live," she says.

Then she is gone, leaving me to ponder what will happen next.

A CUP OF LASSI

A little while later, the aging bird girl is standing at my door, holding out a cup of lassi, the sweet yogurt drink Ama gave me when I was sick.

I take the glass with shaking hands. The drink is sweet and cool and tastes of mango. The girl takes the cup from me, but she remains, watching me.

After a few minutes, I feel odd. And soon her image is fading in and out like lantern light.

I squint and there are two of her. I blink and she is gone.

My arms and legs become distant things, their movements slow and liquid.
Soon the sounds from the bazaar below bleed into one another, a soup of bleating horns and snarling engines.

I try to think. But my thoughts keep collapsing or turning sideways or lapping circles around themselves.

I begin to understand, dimly, that the lassi must have had some strange poison in it, when Mumtaz steps into the room.

After that I don't understand anything.

LUCKY TO BE WITH HABIB

A man with lips like a fish comes into my room and says, "You're lucky to be with Habib." He is squeezing my breast with his hand, like someone shopping for a melon. I try to push him away, but my arm, stone-heavy from the lassi, doesn't move.

"You're lucky," he says, "that Habib is your first one."

I close my eyes. The room pitches this way and that.

"You can tell the others that it was Habib," he says.

I open my eyes, watch him squeeze my other breast, and wonder: Who is this Habib he keeps talking about?

"*If* this is really your first time," he says. "Old Mumtaz is a tricky one."
He unbuckles his belt. "Once before, she sold Habib used goods."

The fish-lips man removes my dress.
I wait for myself to protest. But nothing happens.

"Habib," he says. "Habib is good with the ladies."

Then he is on top of me, and something hot and insistent is between my legs.
He grunts and struggles, trying to fit himself inside me.

With a sudden thrust I am torn in two.

"Oh, yes," he says, panting. "Habib is good in bed."

I hear, coming from a distance,

a steady *thud*,

thud,

thud,

and register that this is the sound of a headboard hitting a wall.

After a while,

I don't know how long,

another sound interrupts the rhythmic thud of the headboard.

I know this noise from somewhere.

I work very hard to make it out.

Finally, I identify it.

It is the muffled sound of sobbing.

Habib rolls off me.

Then I understand: I was the person crying.

ONE OF THEM

I awake stiff and sore. I have no idea of the time,
although I suppose, from the buzzing of the electric sun on
the ceiling, that it is the evening of the next day.

My head throbs. My mouth is parched. I stand on shaky legs,
then collapse on the bare floor, the pain between my legs like
a searing coal.

I grab the bedsheet, struggle to my feet, and make my way to
the little table, where someone has left a glass of water.

Then I catch sight of a girl in the mirror.
She has blackened tiger eyes and bleary chili pepper lips.

She looks back at me full of sadness and scorn and says,
You have become one of them.

TWILIGHT

In the days that follow, many people come to my room.
Some are real. Some are not.

Mumtaz appears each day at dusk and forces a cup of lassi between my clenched jaws. Shahanna comes each morning with a cup of water and face of pity.

They are real. Of that I have no doubt.

In the endless twilight after the lassi, and before the morning, others come.

My stepfather appears, wearing his big-shoulders coat and city hat, puffing on a cigarette. Then Baija Sita is standing at the foot of the bed, locked in gossip with the headman's wife. And sometimes, Auntie Bimla comes, her eyes glinting like new coins.

They seem real, but I know that they are not.

In between, men come.
They crush my bones with their weight.
They split me open.
Then they disappear.

I cannot tell which of the things they do to me are real,
and which are nightmares.

I decide to think that it is all a nightmare.
Because if what is happening is real,
it is unbearable.

HURT

I hurt.

I am torn and bleeding where the men have been.

I pray to the gods to make the hurting go away.

To make the burning and the aching and the bleeding stop.

Music and laughter come from the room next door.

Horns and shouting come from the street below.

No one can hear me.

Not even the gods.

BETWEEN TWILIGHTS

Sometimes, between the twilights,
I unwrap my bundle from home
and bury my face in the fabric of my old skirt.

I inhale deeply,
drinking in the scent of mountain sunshine,
a warmth that smells of freshly turned soil and clean laundry
baking in the sun.
I breathe in a cool Himalayan breeze,
and the woodsy tang of a cooking fire,
a smell that crackles with the promise of warm tea
and fresh roti.

Then I can get by.
Until the next twilight.

WHAT YOU HEAR

Before it starts,
you hear a zipper baring its teeth,
perhaps the sound of a shoe being kicked aside in haste,
the wincing of the mattress.

Once it starts,
you may hear the sound of horns bleating in the street
below,
the peanut vendor hawking his treats,
or the *pock* of a rubber ball as the children shout and play
in the school yard nearby.

But if you are lucky,
or if you work hard at it,
you hear nothing.

Nothing, perhaps, but the clicking of the fan overhead,
the steady ticking away of seconds
until it is over.

Until it starts again.

THE DANGER OF PROTECTION

One day Shahanna comes to my room, bearing a cup of tea and a leftover heel of bread. She slips a small plastic package into my hand.

"Don't let Mumtaz see this," she whispers.

"What is it?" I ask.

She checks to make sure no one can hear.
"A condom."

I don't understand what this condom is and why it must be kept so secret.

Shahanna explains.
"Ask the men to use it, so that you do not get a disease," she says.
"Most of them will say no; they will threaten to go somewhere else if you insist."

I nod.
Shahanna turns to lock the door.

"Do not insist," Shahanna says.
"Or Mumtaz will beat you half to death."

A BUCKET OF WATER

There is a bucket of water next to my bed.

But no matter how often I wash
and scrub
and wash
and scrub,
I cannot seem to rinse the men from my body.

COUNTING

The season has changed.

I only know this because the people outside my window have begun to shed their sweaters. And still I am locked in this room.

The lassi has made my brain too hazy to keep track of how many men have been here.
I do not know how much they pay.
All I know is that each time one leaves, my debt to Mumtaz grows a little smaller.

A HANDFUL OF FOG

I remember the velvet of Tali's pink nose.
The ghostly fragrance of night flowers.
The rough-edged notch in the school bench.
The sunset red of Nepali dirt.
The tinkling music of Ama's earrings.
The silver-white sheen of the mountain in moonlight.

At first, these recollections came unbidden.
Soon, though, I had to work to recall them.
But eventually, with much tracing and retracing,
they became threadbare, thin as the blanket on my bed,
until one day my heart nearly stopped when I could not
summon them up.

Now I practice these memories each morning and night,
the way my teacher taught me to drill my maths.

Still, there is one image that I cannot forget, no matter how
I try.
One stubborn memory that nudges the others out of my head:
Ama's face as she imagined the comfort of a tin roof.

Trying to remember, I have learned,
is like trying to clutch a handful of fog.
Trying to forget,
like trying to hold back the monsoon.

CHANGES

One afternoon, Mumtaz comes to the door and tells me to gather up my things.

"Now that you are no longer a virgin," she says, "I cannot fetch a good price for you."

I cannot believe my ears.
"So I can go now?" I say.

Mumtaz spits.
"You did not come easily," she says. "You cannot easily go."

I don't understand.

"You can go home . . ."
She pauses, picks a fleck of betel leaf off her tongue, examines it.

I try to slow the pounding of my heart at the mention of the word "home."

Mumtaz flicks the bit of leaf into the air and continues.
". . . as soon as you've worked off the twenty thousand rupees I paid for you."

"But—" I have seen her record book, with its entry of 10,000 rupees.
I know this 20,000 price is a lie.

Somehow, of all the things that have been done to me,
this—this outrage—is the worst.

I haven't cried, not one tear, since that first night with the fish-lips man.
But now tears surge up in my eyes.

I blink them back and lift my chin.

"But what?" she says. She pulls the leather strap out from under her skirt and slaps it against her open palm.

I bow my head.

"From now on," Mumtaz says, "you will join the other girls downstairs each night. You will share a bedroom and be free to walk the house."

I stare straight ahead.

Mumtaz comes close and takes my chin in her hand.
"But if you try to run away," she says, "I will grind hot chilies and put them in your private parts."

I shudder, cup my hands over myself, and nod.

"Now hurry up," she says as she walks out. "I need this room."

NEW GIRL

I am gathering up my bowl and my bundle when the aging
bird girl comes in.
With her is another girl, a much younger girl. She is wearing a
bright yellow dress and clutching a bundle of rough homespun
clothes in her arms.

I move toward the door with the halting steps of an old
woman.
It has been a lifetime, it seems, since I was outside this room.
I attempt a first step into the hallway, then another, and
watch as the new girl enters my old room with tentative
steps, as if she is clenching her feet inside her new shoes like
a poor frightened bat clinging to a branch.

WHAT IS NORMAL

The aging bird girl says I am to go to the kitchen, to join the other girls for the midday meal. How odd it is then, after all these days of dreaming to be free, that my feet will not obey.

"Come on," she says.
Then she pinches my ear and drags me into the hall.

The strangeness of walking—moving more than a few paces to the window and back—makes the journey of a dozen steps feel like a million. And the hallway, a stretch of bare floor and cracked walls, seems to me wonderful, new and foreign and vast, and strange. And painfully bright.

When I finally reach the end of the hall, I see a kitchen. Girls in loud, colored dresses are calling out to each other—some in city language, some in my native tongue—all of them shouting to be heard over the wail of a music machine.

They bare their teeth as they laugh, shove handfuls of rice into painted mouths.
A fat, toothless woman stirs a vat of greasy stew while a naked child crawls at her feet, and the air is thick with the smells of spices and cooking oil, perfume and cigarette smoke.

It is all, suddenly, too much.

I sink to the floor, wincing at the tenderness between my thighs.

Then Shahanna is at my side with a steaming bowl of rice. I eat, but do not taste it.

I open my mouth—to thank her, to try to tell her how odd it is to be with people again—but I can't find any words. When I have finished my rice, she helps me to my feet, then says I must come watch TV with everyone else.

"It's fun," she says. "You'll see."

When we get to the TV room, the frowning girl is pushing the button. The box comes to life, just like before. Strange words appear on the glass, and loud, happy music plays. The girls cheer.

"It's *The Bold and the Beautiful*," says Shahanna. "It's from America. It's our favorite show."

Inside the TV, a little pink-skinned man is talking to a woman with hair the color of straw. She raises her hand to slap him across the face, but he catches her wrist in his grip and stops her. Then, without warning, they are kissing.

The Happiness House girls clap and cheer and cackle like hens.

The tiny pink-skinned TV man and woman are strange to me. But these flesh-and-blood girls are, to me, stranger still.

How they can eat and laugh and carry on as normal when soon the men will come is so perplexing that, while they laugh, I fight back tears.

IN MY NEW ROOM

There are posters of gods and movie stars on the walls, an electric sun hanging from the middle of the ceiling, a palm frond machine that stirs the air, a hole-in-the-floor privy, iron bars on the windows, and four rope beds separated by old sheets that hang from the ceiling.

"You draw the sheet around your bed when you have a customer," Shahanna tells me.

Six of us share a room: the half-frowning girl, whose name is Anita; a coughing woman named Pushpa; and her two children. One of the children is a toddler, who is crawling around on the floor dragging an empty plastic bottle on a string. The other, Shahanna says, is a boy of eight.

She points to the half-frowning girl. "Anita," she says, "is from our country."

I place my palms together at my heart and say hello to her in our language. She looks over at me briefly, then goes back to pasting a movie star picture above her bed. I cannot tell, from her crooked face, if she is smiling or frowning. Or both. Or neither.

The coughing woman, Pushpa, came to work for Mumtaz when her husband died. She is pretty—with dusky skin and almond eyes—but she is so thin her collarbones poke out of her dress like the twigs of the neem tree.

As Shahanna is speaking, Pushpa is seized with a bout of coughing that racks her entire body. When the coughing subsides, she spits into a handkerchief, sighs heavily, then curls up on her bed with her face toward the wall. The little girl tugs on Pushpa's braid and cries, "Mama, Mama," but Pushpa doesn't answer.

MEETING THE DAVID BECKHAM BOY

In the middle of the afternoon, a boy of about eight comes in and flings a backpack in the corner. He has hair that sticks up like the tassels on a cornstalk and knees as knobby as a baby goat's. He gives Pushpa a kiss on the cheek and tickles baby Jeena under her chin.

He notices me and points to his shirt. It has the number twenty-three on the back. "David Beckham," he says.

I do not understand these words, but it is clear that this David Beckham boy is very proud of his shirt.

Shahanna says it is time for us to put on our makeup. Pushpa rises wearily, gives the baby a bottle, and puts her on a little bedroll under her cot. The David Beckham boy grabs a paper kite and runs off.

If I could speak his language, I would ask him if the night air in the city smells like the night air on the mountain, like rain clouds and jasmine and possibility.

EVERYTHING I NEED TO KNOW NOW

While Anita and Pushpa stand in front of the mirror, painting their faces, Shahanna explains everything to me.

Before, when you were in the locked room, Shahanna says, Mumtaz sent the customers to you. Now, if you want to pay off your debt, you must do what it takes to make them choose you.

Tell the customers that you are twelve, she says. Or Mumtaz will beat you senseless.

Do whatever the customer asks of you, Shahanna says.
Otherwise he will beat you senseless.
Then he will do whatever he likes and leave without paying.

Always wash yourself with a wet rag after the man is finished, Pushpa says.
This will keep you from getting a disease.

If a customer likes you, he may give you a sweet, she says.
You must eat it right away. Or Mumtaz will take it and eat it herself.

If a customer likes you, he may give you a tip. Hide it where no one can see so that you will have enough to buy yourself a cup of tea each day.

Once a month, Pushpa says, a government woman comes to the back door with a basket of condoms. Take a handful and hide them under your mattress, but do not let Shilpa, the aging bird girl, see you; she is Mumtaz's spy.

The Americans will try to trick you into running away, says Anita. Don't be fooled. They will shame you and make you walk naked through the streets.

If an old man is at the door, bat your eyelashes and act the part of a little girl, says Pushpa. He will pay extra for this.

If Mumtaz brings you one of her important friends, bat your eyelashes and act the part of a little girl, says Shahanna. He will pay nothing.

There are special things you need to know about how to use your shawl, she says.
Flick the ends of your shawl in a come-closer gesture and you will bring the shy men to your bed, the ones who will slip an extra coin into your hand before they go.

Draw your shawl to your chin, bend your neck like a peacock. This will bring the older men to your bed, the ones who will leave a sweet on your pillow.

Press your shawl to your nose with the back of your hand,

Pushpa says, when you must bring a dirty man to your bed. He will leave nothing but his smell, the stink of sweat, and hair oil and liquor and man. But you can use your shawl to block the worst of it.

Anita turns away from the mirror, transformed from a crooked-faced country girl into a tiger-eyed city woman.

There is another way to use a shawl, she says.

I cannot tell from her always-frowning face if she is being kind or cruel.

That new girl, the one in your old room, she says. Yesterday morning Mumtaz found her hanging from the rafters.

PRETENDING

Her coughing is so bad today that Pushpa cannot get out of bed, so we take turns playing with baby Jeena, tickling her, cooing to her, bouncing her on our knees. It is peaceful until Anita and the cook begin pinching each other's ears over whose turn it is to hold the baby. In the midst of their fighting the baby begins to wail.

Pushpa rises wearily from her cot and takes Jeena in her arms. "You do not remember," she whispers to her little girl, "but we used to have a proper home." She opens her blouse and puts the child to her breast. But it is to no avail. There is no nourishment left in Pushpa's withered body, and again the baby begins to cry.

Jeena is not the only baby here. Several of the women have children. They dote on them, going even deeper into debt with Mumtaz to buy them fresh clothes for school, hair ribbons, and sneakers. The others—the ones without children—treat them like pets, buying them sweets from the street boy when one of their good customers gives them a tip.

I ask Shahanna why this is so.

"We all need to pretend," she says. "If we did not pretend, how would we live?"

"But why does Mumtaz go along with this?"

"Only Mumtaz does not pretend," she says. "She knows that once the women have children, they cannot leave. They will do whatever she asks, or be thrown out in the street."

I ask Shahanna why the women don't get the shots that will keep the babies from coming.

She looks at me like I'm mad. "All the girls want babies," she says. "It's our only family here."

And so the children of Happiness House go off to school in the mornings and come home in the afternoons and do their homework. They play tag in the alleyway, eat sweet cakes, and watch TV.

But in the evening, it is harder to pretend. As soon as dark falls, the bigger ones go up to the roof. They fly homemade paper kites until they are too tired to stand, daring to come down to sleep only late at night after the men have finally gone. The younger ones, like Jeena, are given special medicine so they can sleep under the bed while their mothers are with customers.

Morning comes early for the children at Happiness House, and they beg for more sleep with dazed and cloudy eyes. It takes a great deal of coaxing to get them dressed in their school clothes to begin another day of pretending.

THE CUSTOMERS

They are old, young, dirty, clean, tall, short, dark, light, bearded, smooth, fat, thin.

They are all the same.

Most of them are from the city.
A few are from my home country.

One day, a customer addressed his friend in my language as they left.
"How was yours?" he said. "Was she good?"

"It was great," the other one said. "I wish I could do it again."

"Me, too," said the first one. "If only I had another thirty rupees."

Thirty rupees.

That is the price of a bottle of Coca-Cola at Bajai Sita's store.

That is what he paid for me.

MATHEMATICS

In the village school we were taught to add, subtract, multiply, and divide.

The teacher gave us difficult problems, asking us to figure out how many baskets of rice a family would have to sell to buy a new water buffalo. Or how many lengths of fabric a mother would need to make a vest and pants for her husband and still have enough for a dress for her baby. I would chew on the ends of my braids while my mind whirred, desperate to come up with the answer that would spread a smile on her soft moon face.

Here I do a different set of calculations.

If I bring a half dozen men to my room each night, and each man pays Mumtaz 30 rupees, I am 180 rupees closer each day to going back home. If I work for a hundred days more, I should have nearly enough to pay back the 20,000 rupees I owe to Mumtaz.

Then Shahanna teaches me city subtraction.

Half of what the men pay goes to Mumtaz, she says. Then you must take away 80 rupees for what Mumtaz charges for your daily rice and dal. Another 100 a week for renting you a bed and pillow. And 500 for the shot the dirty-hands doctor gives us once a month so that we won't become pregnant.

She also warns me: Mumtaz will bury you alive if she sees your little book of figures.

I do the calculations.

And realize I am already buried alive.

MONICA

There is one girl here who gets the most customers. She is not the prettiest among us—she has a face like a fox and pointy gray teeth—but she is the boldest. While the rest of us wait for the men to point in our direction, Monica trains her hungry eyes on them the minute they walk in the door.

She does not bat her eyelashes and act the little girl. She preens and struts and twines her arms around the men like a thirsty vine.

One night, I am alone with Monica. She is studying one of her beloved movie magazines, posing and puckering her lips like the woman on the page in front of her.

"I can teach you some tricks," she says to me. "Tricks to make the customers pay more."

I am afraid of this thirsty-vine woman. I look at my hands folded in my lap, and say nothing.

"You think you are better than me?" she says. "Too good to learn my tricks?"

I am too afraid to even shake my head no.

"Hah!" She laughs mirthlessly, tossing her hair over her shoulder with a shake of her head. "I've earned nearly

enough to pay down my debt," she says.
"In another month, I'll be on my way home."

I try to take in this idea—that Monica will soon be free—when a man comes into the room. He has city shoes on his feet and a gold chain around his neck. In an instant, Monica is at his side, winding her arms around him, like a snake.

And then they are gone, and I am alone to consider an odd and somewhat sour feeling: disappointment that the man did not choose me.

AN ORDINARY BOY

I have been watching the David Beckham boy, although I do not let on.

I know that the first thing he does when he comes home from school is to kiss Pushpa and tickle his baby sister.
I know that he sticks his tongue out when he is concentrating on his homework.
I know that Anita saves her bread for him since she cannot chew on her bad side.
I know that he has two favorite television shows: one where men kick a black-and-white ball around a giant green paddy field, and another where people try to guess the right answers to difficult questions so they can win a million rupees. And I know that he plays along with the millionaire show, because I saw him whispering the answers under his breath.
I know that he keeps his belongings in a tin trunk under his bed. And I know what's in there—a rusty key, an empty bottle of hair oil, a plastic flower, and three gold buttons—because I peeked inside when he was at school one day.

I know, from all this watching, that he is just an ordinary boy.

But sometimes I find myself hating him.
I hate him for having schoolbooks and playmates.
For having a mother who combs his hair on the mornings

she's feeling well enough.
And for having the freedom to come and go as he pleases.

But sometimes, I hate myself for hating him.
Simply because he *is* an ordinary boy.

WHAT IS MISSING NOW

I no longer notice the smell of the indoor privy.
And I long ago stopped feeling the blows of Mumtaz's strap.

But today when I buried my face in my bundle of clothes
from home, there was no hearth smoke in the folds of my
skirt, no crisp Himalayan night air in my shawl.

I have been frugal with myself, not daring to unwrap the
bundle more than once a day, for fear that it would lose
its magic.

But today, it became just a rag skirt and a tattered shawl.

STEALING FROM THE DAVID BECKHAM BOY

It seems that the David Beckham boy runs a business here.

In the afternoons, he runs errands. The good-earning girls, the ones who are allowed to keep their tips, give him a list of what they want and send him out to the stores. I have seen him come back with movie magazines for Monica and Coca-Cola for Shilpa. Sometimes he just gets a smeary lipstick kiss on the cheek. But sometimes he gets a few coins for his troubles.

At night, he works for their customers. They yell for him, and he runs to the corner to get them liquor or cigarettes. Sometimes he gets nothing more than a pat on the head. And sometimes, if he takes too long, a slap across the face. But sometimes he gets a rupee or two.

When he thinks no one is looking, he hides his earnings in his little tin trunk.

In the afternoons, when he is out playing tag with his school chums or running his errand business, I steal from the David Beckham boy.

I do not take his money, though. I steal something better.

While the other girls are downstairs watching the TV, I take his brightly colored storybook and make it mine.

I do not understand the words inside, and the pictures are queer and otherwordly.

But at least for a few minutes, I pretend I am in school with Gita and my soft, moonfaced teacher, and I am the number one girl in class again.

UNDERSTANDING ANITA

I ask Shahanna why Anita is always frowning.

"She is angry all the time," I say. "Even when *The Bold and the Beautiful* is on TV."

"Anita escaped once," Shahanna says. "When the goondas found her, they beat her with a metal pipe."

I don't know this word *goonda.*

"The goondas are men who work for Mumtaz," she says. "If you try to escape, they will hunt you. If they catch you, they will beat you. If you get a disease, they will throw you out in the street. If you try to get back in, they will beat you."

I ask Shahanna what happened to Anita.

"The goondas smashed her cheek and her jaw. Now one side of her face is dead. She could not smile, even if she had a reason to."

REMOTE CONTROL

Shahanna has explained that there is a box Anita uses to
operate the TV.
If she pushes one button, the people inside get louder.
If she pushes another, they get quiet.
Sometimes, if Mumtaz has a headache, Anita pushes another
button, and the TV people make no noise at all.

The most important button is the red one. This one can
make the TV people appear.
Or disappear.

Sometimes, I pretend that what goes on at night when the
customers are here is not something that is happening to
me. I pretend it is a TV show that I am watching from far, far
away. I pretend I have a button I press to make everything
go quiet. And another one that makes me disappear.

CAUGHT

One afternoon, I linger too long in my make-believe school, and the David Beckham boy catches me poring over his storybook.

I drop the book to the floor and wait for him to pull my hair or rap my knuckles.

But he just cocks his head to one side and stares at me. He steps close and stoops to pick up the book. He holds it out in my direction. But I turn my back to him and flee the room, pounding the floor with my heels as I go.

I hate him more than ever now.
For catching me at my make-believe game.
For seeing that I want his life for my own.

And for the pity in his eyes as he offered to share it with me.

POLICE

Tonight I saw a curious thing. Usually the men give their money to Mumtaz. What I saw tonight, as I came downstairs, was Mumtaz handing a fat roll of rupee notes to a man.

He was dressed all in tan, like the man at the border, and he had a gun on his hip. While the man was counting his money, Shilpa, the aging bird girl who spies for Mumtaz, spotted me and chased me away.

"Is that man a goonda?" I ask Shahanna.

"He's worse," she says. "He's a policeman."

I don't understand.

"Policemen are supposed to stop people like Mumtaz from selling girls," she says. "But she gives this one money each week and he looks the other way."

I don't understand this city. It is full of so many bad people. Even the people who are supposed to be good.

NO ORDINARY BOY, AFTER ALL

My new custom is to wait by the window each afternoon so that I can see the David Beckham boy coming home from school. That way, I can put his book back in its hiding place before he arrives.

What I usually see first is whatever he is kicking ahead of him—a lemon rind or a rotten onion from the trash heap. He pretends it is a ball, like the black-and-white one on the TV show he likes so much.

Today when I see him, he has had the good fortune to find a rotten melon. Melons seem to be his favorite, since they make a wonderful mess when they strike the curb.

He is sticking his tongue out ever so slightly—the way he does when he is concentrating on his math—as he nudges the melon in and out of the ruts in the road. And so he doesn't see the older boys—the ones who chase the pariah dogs with stones—waiting across the street from Happiness House.

I do not understand what they say to him. But they are smiling and tugging at the hem of his David Beckham shirt.

He offers them an eager smile and shows them how he can balance the melon on the tip of his toe.

They seem to be impressed. At least for a moment.

Then they are pinching his ear and jabbing at his David Beckham shirt. I cannot understand what they say, but I know the word they hurl at him again and again. It is a dirty word, one the customers yell when they are drunk or angry. They are calling his ama a whore.

The David Beckham boy looks furtively toward the front door, where Pushpa waits for him on the days she feels well enough. I duck inside, but not before I see him stuff his hands in his pants pockets and walk away, leaving that sweet, rotten melon abandoned by the curb.

SOMETHING ELSE I KNOW ABOUT THE DAVID BECKHAM BOY

I know that lately, when he bends to kiss his ama each afternoon, he lingers longer than he used to.

I know that he is checking for a fever.

I know because I overheard Mumtaz telling Pushpa that if the fever comes back, they will all be out on the street.

YES

I am sitting on my bed, adding yesterday's profits to the tally in my notebook, when the David Beckham boy comes in. My old yellow pencil is nothing but a stub, and I slip it up my sleeve so this boy who goes to a proper school and does his work with a proper pencil won't see.

He grabs his kite and turns to leave, then stops a moment and looks at me.

"Do you want me to teach you how to read the words in the storybook?" he says.

I do.
I don't dare admit how much.

"Yes," I say, my eyes still fixed on my notebook.
"Yes, I do."

"Okay, then," he says. "I'll give you a lesson when I get home from school tomorrow."

And then he is gone. Leaving me to consider how long it has been since a tomorrow meant anything to me.

WHAT I LEARNED TODAY

When the David Beckham boy came home from school today, he threw his backpack in the corner, kissed his mother, played with his sister, and then sat down and taught me a few important things.

I learned that there are two languages here: Hindi and English.
I learned that Hindi is not too different from my native tongue.

I learned the Hindi words for:
girl,
boy,
and "*How are you today?*"

MORE WORDS

Today the David Beckham boy taught me some more words.

Now I can say:

sit,

walk,

book,

bowl,

good,

bad,

happy,

and *sad.*

I learned some sentences, too:

"*My name is Lakshmi.*"

"*I am from Nepal.*"

"*I am thirteen.*"

I also learned that the David Beckham boy's name is Harish.

David Beckham, it seems, is some kind of god.

TWO WORLDS

Today the TV will not work, and the girls beg Monica and Shilpa to tell us a movie. Monica seems vexed by this request, but it is an act, Shahanna tells me. Monica loves the movies more than anything in the world.

And so we sit at Monica's feet as she tells us about a wealthy bride who opposed the marriage her parents had arranged. The bride ran off to a festival and fell in love with a handsome boy. They sang and danced and ran in and out of the rain. Until the bride's father found her and dragged her home.

The day of the wedding, the bride cried bitter tears as the guests threw marigolds at her feet. The groom rode into the wedding tent on a white horse. And still the bride wept. Until she saw that it was the boy from the festival. And they sang and danced with the mother and father to celebrate the happy love match.

The other girls have a hundred questions.
How do they make it rain in a movie?
How many marigolds did they use? A hundred? A thousand?
Did the horse wear a saddle of gold?

I have only one question:
"How do Monica and Shilpa know about the movies?"
I whisper to Shahanna.

"Sometimes Mumtaz lets the good-earning girls go to the movies," she says.

"They don't run away?"

"Shilpa is here of her own choice," says Shahanna. "She has no debt to Mumtaz. She can leave any time she likes."

I don't understand.

"Her mother was in this business and now she is in the business. It is the family trade."

"And Monica?"

"Monica is going home in a month or so."

"But still, she could run away before paying off her debt," I say.

"They say Monica has a child at home." Shahanna says. "If she runs off, Mumtaz will take the child."

"What would Mumtaz want with a child?"

"She will maim it—cut off a hand, a foot—and sell it to a beggar woman," she says. "Softhearted people will give an extra rupee or two if you have a sick baby."

And so I consider a world so ugly that a child would be maimed for life to fetch an extra rupee or two. And another world full of brides and marigolds, rain machines and white horses.

THE STREET BOY

Other than the old vegetable peddler, the street boy who sells tea from a wire caddy is the only visitor who comes here during the day.

He has barely a whisker on his face, and he is skinny and dirty, but the girls tease him and flirt with him and tell them they will trade him kisses for tea. He flirts and jokes in return, but never goes to their beds.

I am watching his antics today when he turns to me. "Why do you never buy my tea?" he asks in my language.

I am too shy to answer. If I weren't, I would tell him that I am saving all my money so that someday I can go home. But I am ashamed to have this boy from my country see me in this shameful place, and so I flee the room and say nothing.

WHAT I LEARNED TODAY

My notebook is nearly full. There are the old equations that my mountain teacher gave me. There are the odd new words I learned on my journey with Uncle Husband. There are pages of calculations, showing my debt to Mumtaz and my earnings so far.

And now there are pages full of the Hindi and English words Harish has taught me. Beautiful words like:

candy,
bread,
cricket,
pen,
crayon,
dress,
bracelet,
radio,
chicken,
cow,
cartoon,
and *remote control.*

Shahanna comes in and sees me writing in my notebook. "Don't let Mumtaz or Shilpa see you with that," she says.

"If they find out you can read and write, they will think you are planning to escape."

I nod.

"And then they will put you back in the locked-in room."

SHILPA'S SECRET

Today on my way to the kitchen, I pass by the counting room and see Shilpa buying a bottle of liquor from the street boy. Her hands are trembling as she gives him the money. She swallows half the bottle in one long gulp, then tells the boy to be on his way. He looks at me with furtive eyes as he runs past, and when Shilpa sees me watching, she spits at me and tells me to mind my own business.

Later, I ask Shahanna why Shilpa would drink that hateful liquid.

"She likes it," she says.

I don't understand.

"Her mother gave it to her when she was young, so it would not hurt so much when she was with a customer. She says she used to hate it. But now she likes it too much."

HOW ARE YOU TODAY?

Whenever Harish sees me, he says, in the new language I am learning, "*How are you today?*"

I reply, "*Fine, thank you. And you?*"

I love the way these new words feel in my mouth.
Even if they are not true.

A STRANGE VOCABULARY

Now Harish is teaching me American words from a new storybook. The book was a present from a white woman who runs a special singing-and-playing school where Harish goes on Saturdays.

He says the American lady is kind. He says Anita is wrong about the Americans, that they do not shame the children of the brothels. He says this is a story Mumtaz has told her to keep her from running away.

I do not know which of them to believe.

But I do know, from this storybook, that this America is a strange place.

Everyone there is as rich as a king.
The birds there are big as men.
They eat a sweet treat made from snow.
And the children play the kicking game with the black-and-white ball, like the one on TV.
This is the David Beckham game, Harish says.

These are the American words I can say:

Big Bird,

Elmo,

ice cream,

soccer.

DON'T CROSS THE COOK

Today I learn a new Hindi sentence: "*Don't cross the cook or she will spit in your soup.*"

Harish says this with a very serious face, and at first I don't recognize the word *cook*.
So he uses his hands to make a stirring gesture. I still don't get the meaning.
And so he draws the shape of a fat-bottomed woman in his notebook. Then he jumps up, puffs out his stomach, and stomps around the room, his skinny little-boy legs pounding out a perfect imitation of her thundering walk.

"*Cook!*" I cry out at last.

Harish throws back his head and laughs.

And I laugh, too.

It is strange to laugh after all these months, odd and unfamiliar. But somehow, not hard at all.

AN ACCIDENTAL KINDNESS

The man who came to my room today was not like the others. He was young and clean and gentle.

He did not simply stand and zip his trousers when he was finished, or fall heavily asleep on top of me the way some do. He didn't fix his hair in the mirror and walk out without a word.

He held me.

Perhaps it was an accident. Or perhaps he forgot where he was, imagining for a moment he was with his sweetheart.

But I could feel myself, my true self, give in to the simple pleasure of being held. His body warmed mine the way the Himalayan sun warms the soil. His skin was soft—like the velvet of Tali's nose. And his contentment soaked through to me like an evening rain shower.

And so I held him, too.

Slowly, I put my arms around him and allowed them to stay.

Eventually, we pulled apart. I was the last to let go.

He stood and looked at me with something like shyness. "Thank you," he said.

Harish had taught me how to say thank you in his language, but it seemed a paltry word for my debt to this man.

AM I PRETTY?

In the days after the hugging man leaves, I consider myself in the mirror. My plain self, not the self wearing lipstick and eyeliner and a filmy dress.

Sometimes I see a girl who is growing into womanhood. Other days I see a girl growing old before her time.

It doesn't matter, of course. Because no one will ever want me now.

NOT COUNTING

It has been twelve days since the hugging man came.

I have decided to stop counting the days until he comes back.

UNDERSTANDING MONICA

Everyone here is afraid of Monica's temper. When the cook put a sad song on the music machine, Monica yanked on her braid until she turned it off. When Anita asked if it was true that she had a child back home, Monica pinched her ear until she howled. And when Shahanna entered her room without permission, Monica threw a pair of shoes at her.

But Monica is also given to strange fits of kindness. Once, when the dirty-hands doctor pushed himself up against me in a back hall, Monica pried him off of me and told him he would have to pay like everyone else. And the other day, she gave Anita a bottle of nail polish, saying she wouldn't need it when she goes home next month.

And so when I see her watching TV alone, I slip into the room and sit silently nearby, wondering which Monica she is today.

She regards me, then lights a cigarette. "You know how to write, don't you?"

I do. At home, such a skill is something to boast about. But as Shahanna has told me, here, it is a dangerous thing to admit.

"My little girl can write," she says. "I am paying her school fees."

So it is true, the rumor of Monica's child.

"I paid for her medicine," Monica says, thrusting her pointy chin in the air. "And for an operation for my father. And for a pair of spectacles for my sister."

I raise my chin, too.
"I am buying a new roof for my family," I say.

Monica exhales. "They will thank us," she says. "They will thank us and honor us when we go home."

I dare not picture this, a date so far away that it is like a dream.

"My sister wrote and said my little girl hates porridge," Monica says.

I try to picture this, a feisty little Monica.

"I bet she pinches your sister when she tries to make her eat it," I say.

Monica looks surprised, then she laughs and pinches my ear, ever so slightly, and we go back to watching a TV world full of brides and white horses.

A GIFT

Today, Harish tells me, is the festival of brothers and sisters. He shows me the rag doll he is giving to Jeena. "I bought it with my own money," he says.

Then he hands me a pencil. It is shiny yellow and it smells of lead and rubber. And possibility.

"For you," he says.

And then he runs off, his paper kite in his hand. And I am glad because something strange is happening. Something surprising and unstoppable.

A tear is running down my cheek. It quivers a moment on the tip of my nose, then splashes onto my skirt, leaving a small, dark circle.

I have been beaten here,
locked away,
violated a hundred times
and a hundred times more.
I have been starved
and cheated,
tricked
and disgraced.

How odd it is that I am undone by the simple kindness
of a small boy with a yellow pencil.

SOMETHING FOR THE DAVID BECKHAM BOY

The next day, I am at the window waiting for Harish to return from school. I see him come down the lane, playing make-believe soccer with a tin can. I tap on the windowpane, and a few minutes later I hear him bounding up the steps.

He walks into our room and I offer him my gift: it is a ball of rags, my old homespun shawl, ripped into shreds and tied in a tight round bundle.

He is puzzled at this bundle of ragged cloth.

"A soccer ball," I tell him.

He takes the ball of rags and balances it on his toe. He nods his approval. He nudges it around the room. Then gives it a good, solid kick toward the door frame. He spreads his arms wide, like a bird in flight, and calls back a quick thank you over his shoulder.

Then he is gone. I hear the front door close, and I run to the window to watch him turn into a barefoot David Beckham dodging shoppers and rickshaws as he heads down the lane.

I follow him with my eyes for as long as I can. A piece of me has left Happiness House.

STILL NOT COUNTING

It has been thirty days since the hugging man came.

I have decided that he is not coming back.

WHEN MONICA LEFT

She gave away all her makeup and fancy baubles. She even gave Shahanna the shoes she'd thrown at her. She came to my room to say good-bye, but I hid under the blanket, feigning sleep so she would not see the envy in my heart.

After she left, I found the movie magazine she'd left on my pillow.

That afternoon, the cook put a sad song on the music machine. And we who remain at Happiness House listened all the way through to the end, too unhappy for tears.

SORRY

By the time Harish comes home today, the sun has set and it is already time for me to go to work. But he takes a minute to teach me two new words before going up to the roof to fly his kite.

The first word is *marbles*. He holds out his hand and shows me the colorful glass balls. He explains, I think, that he was late for our lesson because he was playing marbles with his friends at the American lady's school.

The other word is *sorry*. He says he is very sad that we can't have our lesson today. This, he said, is what sorry means.

I ruffle his hair and tell him not to be sad. Anyway, I say, today my head aches too badly to have a lesson.

THE COST OF A CURE

I lie on my cot, drenched in sweat, struggling to wake up.

I slip into a dream, and Gita and are I playing the hopping-on-one-leg game in the dirt path between our huts. She bends, scoops a stone up from one of the squares we've drawn with a stick, then she skips away, her long, black braid swinging side to side, in time with her singsong chant. She turns back and beckons me to follow her. But somehow she has turned into Auntie Bimla singing the same song through black-stained teeth.

I open my eyes and see the place where I live now: a dank room with four beds, four dirty curtains hanging from the ceiling, and iron bars on the windows.

Now I am shaking with cold. I pull the thin sheet around my shoulders, but the trembling goes on. I burrow against the wall, hugging myself, and soon I am sweating again.

It has been like this since last night. Sleeping then waking, fever then chills. Each one in a battle for my body.

Now Harish, in his David Beckham shirt, is standing over me. He puts his hand on my brow. If I could speak, I would beg him to stay with me forever, his cool, cool hand on my forehead. But he disappears.

And I am dreaming again. Of flying—on the wings of his kite—high above the snowy, swallow-tailed peak, while he is on the ground below, letting out more and more string, more and more, until he is just a tiny speck on the ground below.

An angry voice brings me back down to earth. It is Mumtaz.

"Faker," she says. "Get out of bed."

I open my eyes and see her standing over me, with Harish next to her, shaking his head. He puts his hand on my brow again and tells Mumtaz something that makes her frown. She waves a hand at him, like she is swatting at a mosquito, and sends him away.

"Have you been washing yourself?" she says. "After the men. Do you wash yourself down there?"

I try to nod, but my head is heavy, achy, a distant thing I cannot control. All I can do is close my eyes.

Now I am in another bed. A kindly woman in white leans over me, swabbing my head with a cool rag. She tells me she will bring me some of the sweet American treat made from snow, then she disappears.

Now I am climbing out the window of this new place,

sneaking through the streets in my nightdress, past the peanut vendor, past the children playing ball, past the women shopping for fabrics, past the mongrel dogs sniffing through the trash, until I am running, running, running toward home.

"Here," says a voice. "Take these."

I open my eyes.

Mumtaz is standing over me. Mumtaz, with her plump mango face, has taken the place of the kindly woman in white, and she is holding out a pair of white pills.

I understand then, that the woman and her cool cloth and the snowy treat and the running were all a dream.

Mumtaz lifts my head from the pillow, places the pills on my tongue, then brings a glass of water to my lips.

I swallow, and for a moment, I love her.

I love her like a mother, for giving me the medicine that will stop the fever and the sweating and the chills and the shaking. I love her for not throwing me out on the street, for caring for me.

I reach out to thank her, but she is bustling around, putting two more pills on the table next to my bed, refilling my glass of water.

"Take these pills tonight," she says. "And you'll be back at work in no time."

Then she unwinds her waistcloth and takes out her record book. She wets her pencil with the tip of her tongue and writes a number in her book.

"You'll be able to work off the cost of the medicine in a few days," she says.

And then she is gone.

And try as I might, I cannot bring back my dreams.

AN OLD WOMAN

A few days later, when I am finally strong enough to get out of bed, I pass by a mirror. The face that looks back is that of a corpse.

Her eyes are empty. She is old and tired. Old and angry. Old and sad. Old, old, a hundred years old.

I speak to her in the words Harish taught me.

"*My name is Lakshmi*," I tell her. "*I am from Nepal. I am thirteen years old.*"

THE LIVING DEAD

Today at the morning meal, an unfamiliar figure is at the table, hunched over a bowl, picking at her rice. She looks up, and I see that it is Monica.

"Well," she says with strange cheer. "My father recovered from his operation."

Her smile is wide, too wide. And I am afraid of her angry happiness.

"He needs a cane," she says. "But he is still as strong as a goat."

I nod slowly, unsure what to say.

"Look," she says. She shrugs off her shawl, revealing arms and shoulders covered in angry purple bruises. "He did this with his cane."

I wince.
But Monica laughs bitterly.

I don't understand.
"I thought you said they would honor you and thank you," I say.

She snorts.

"When they heard I was coming," she says, "they met me outside the village and begged me not to come back and disgrace them."

"Did you get to see your daughter?" I say.

Monica cannot meet my eyes.

"They told her I was dead."

Pushpa has been in bed for three days and nights, and now Mumtaz is in our room. "If you don't get out of bed and see customers today," she says, "you are out on the street."

Pushpa nods, stands slowly, then sinks to her knees. She kisses Mumtaz's feet.

"Please," she begs. "I'll work tonight, I promise."

Then she is seized by one of her coughing fits. She coughs until tears run down her cheeks and she spits blood into a rag.

"Pshhht," Mumtaz says. "You are of no use to me now! No man wants to make love to walking death."

"Have mercy," Pushpa cries, holding her hands up in prayer. "Think of my children."

Mumtaz sneers at her, then all at once her eyes begin to gleam like new rupee coins.

"There is something you could do," Mumtaz says.

Pushpa looks up expectantly.

"Sell her to me." She points to little Jeena, asleep in her bedroll. "In a few years, when she is old enough, I can make a lot of money with her."

Pushpa seems not to understand.

"There are men who would pay dearly," Mumtaz says, "to be with a pure one. Men who think it will cure their disease."

She puts a hand on Pushpa's slender shoulder and smiles.

Then comes an unearthly sound. It is a wild sound, an animal sound, a howling, mournful, raging cry, as the sickly woman on the floor claws at the skirts of the fat woman standing over her.

It is a sound beyond language.

WHAT DESPAIR LOOKS LIKE

For the rest of the afternoon, Pushpa sits on her bed with her head in her hands. Shahanna tries to comfort her, but Pushpa stares into space, unmoving. Finally she rises, tucks a blanket under Jeena's chin, and whispers to her. "Don't worry," she says. "I will not let that woman take you."

Then Harish comes home from school, flushed and disheveled from his game of make-believe soccer. He beams at his mother, delighted to see her out of bed, then stops as he takes in her misery.

Neither one says a word. Harish simply pulls his little tin trunk out from under the bed, and the two of them begin packing their things.

A WORD TOO SMALL

I look on, speechless, as Harish ties up his bedroll and Pushpa places her possessions—a hairbrush, a sweater, a photo of her husband—inside Harish's trunk.

Anita is sitting on the bed, clutching Jeena to her breast, the two sides of her poor, lopsided face matched, for once, in perfect misery. Finally, Anita kisses the top of the baby's head, hands her to Pushpa, then runs from the room, sobbing.

Harish looks up at me.
"*How are you today, Lakshmi?*" he says.
The words are the same as always; but his little-boy voice breaks as he says my name.

I am not fine. I cannot pretend. But I do not know a word big enough to hold my sadness.
I bite my lip and shrug.

Harish looks away, then goes back to his packing.

"Where will you go?" I say.

"I will ask the lady teacher from America if she knows a place we can stay until my mother is better," he says. "Until then, I must earn the money."

He places his rag-bundle soccer ball inside the trunk, snaps it shut. "I have heard they pay children fifty rupees a week," he says, "to break stones at the roadside."

He lifts the trunk, his skinny arms straining at the weight, and I wonder how long those little arms will last breaking stones.

I point to the American storybook he's left.
"Don't forget this."

He shifts the trunk to his other arm.
"You can have it," he says.

Harish walks to the door, dragging the trunk.

All the words he taught me, all the beautiful words, are useless now.

Finally I remember one, one that will answer the question he asked—"How are you today, Lakshmi?"—as if today were just another day.

"Harish," I say.

He just looks at me.

"*Sorry,*" I say. "*I am sorry today.*"

Then he is gone.

REPETITION

"*Lakshmi*," I say to myself. "*My name is Lakshmi*."

Now that Harish is gone, no one says my name.

So I say it to myself. "*My name is Lakshmi*," I repeat.
"*I am from Nepal.*
I am thirteen."

I am not sure, but I think so much time has passed, that
I am fourteen.

LIKE ANITA

In the afternoons now, I watch TV with my head on
Shahanna's shoulder. But without Harish, I am like Anita.
I cannot smile, even if there is a reason.

INSTEAD OF HARISH

Monica comes to my room today, her hands behind her back.

"Are the others all downstairs?" she whispers.

I nod. It is time for *The Bold and the Beautiful.* The others would all be laughing and cheering, while I lie upstairs in my bed pretending that Harish will be home any minute to resume our lessons.

"Here," she says. "Take this."
She thrusts a tattered, gray thing in my direction.

I examine it cautiously and see that it is an old rag doll, loved almost beyond recognition. Its button eyes are gone. Its mouth, a tiny red stitch. Its dress thin and colorless.

"You can have her for a while," she says. "You know, instead of Harish."

She says this so quickly her words barely register.

I stand to thank her but she is already gone.

And I understand then, somehow, that Monica, the thirsty vine, Monica, the one with tricks to make the men pay extra, sleeps with this tattered rag doll.

A STRANGE CUSTOMER

I have never seen such a queer-looking person. He has the pink skin of a pig. His hair is the color of straw. His eyes are ice blue. And he is wearing short pants that show his hairy monkey legs. But he looks like one of the people in Harish's storybook.

He is too friendly, this pink American man. He grips my hand in greeting, a strange and uncouth gesture that makes me pull back in alarm.

He says hello in my language.

I say nothing in reply.

"What is your name?" he says.

His words are slow and clumsy, as if he has a mouth full of roti.

"Your name," he says again, more slowly still. "What is your name?"

This pink man is the first man here to ask my name, but I don't give it to him.

"How old are you?"

I know what I am supposed to say. But something keeps me

from lying to this pink stranger. I shrug.

He is unmoved by my rudeness. Indeed, he smiles, his ice-blue eyes oddly warm.

"Are you being kept here against your will?"

My will? This is something I lost long ago, I want to tell him.

I want to pummel this pink-skinned man with my fists.
I want to spit on this stranger with his eyes of cold pity,
his idiot way of speaking my language, and his bad-mannered
questions that make me look at the humiliation that is my life.

I fold my arms across myself.

He takes a little book from one of his pockets, consults its battered pages, then looks up at me. Slowly, with care, he asks me a question.

"Do you want to leave here?"

I know about these Americans. Anita has told me all about them. I will not be fooled into leaving here only to be stripped naked and have people throw stones at me and call me a dirty woman.

I shake my head no.

"You don't want to leave here?"

I just stare at him.

"I can take you to a place where you will get new clothes," he says. "And good food. And you will not have to be with men."

I pretend I don't understand. Because I don't.
I don't understand how I will pay my debt to Mumtaz in this new place.

"Do you want to go there?"

I shake my head no.

"It is a clean place," he says.

I don't even blink.

He takes his wallet from his jacket. I wait to catch a glimpse of his riches, but what he hands me is a small white card. It is full of American words I cannot read, and in the center is a drawing of a bird in flight.

I put the card inside my waistcloth.
And then he is gone.

How odd he is, this man who pays for a girl and does nothing but talk.

A SMALL DANGER

I study the strange American card. It has words and numbers
in tiny print.
It is a small thing, flimsy and light, but I know it is enough to
earn me a beating if Mumtaz or Shilpa sees it.

If I put it in the trash in the kitchen, the others will see.
If I throw it out the window, Mumtaz might see.

And so I take this dangerous card and hide it under the mat
on the floor.
Until I can think of a better way to get rid of it.

And then I head back downstairs and try to forget all about
my strange visitor.

A SECRET

There is a moment, between the light and the dark, when the smell of frying onions blows in through the windows. All over the city, the cooking hour has begun. This is the saddest smell in the world because it means that here at Mumtaz's house the men will start to arrive.

I am looking out the window, my whole being yearning toward that smell, when Shahanna comes in.

"Shahanna," I say. "Can you keep a secret?"

She looks around to make sure that we are alone and nods. "I had an American customer the other day," I say. "He said he would take me away from here."

Shahanna moves a step closer to me, her dark eyes narrowed with suspicion.

"Did he say he would pay off your debt to Mumtaz?"

I shake my head.

"Then how would you get past her goondas?"

"I don't know," I say.

"You know what Anita says," she whispers. "She says the Americans will trick you and shame you and make you walk naked in public."

I nod. I think about telling her what he said about the clean place, about the new clothes he promised. "Perhaps," I say, "Anita is wrong."

Shahanna looks out the window at the street below. "But Anita's the only one of us who's been out there," she says.

We are both quiet for a moment, watching the world outside go by underneath our window bars.

Then Shahanna grasps my hands in hers. "If he comes back, will you go with him?" she says.

I don't know what to say.

She squeezes my hands tightly, and her eyes burn with a fervor I have never seen before in my gentle friend. "Will you take me with you?"

I step back. Shahanna has been nothing but kind to me, from the day I first arrived. She taught me everything I know to survive here. But she scares me now with this wild talk.

I am afraid. Afraid that Mumtaz will beat us senseless. And I am afraid that the Americans will shame us and abandon us in the streets.

But most of all, I am afraid to imagine a life outside this place.

POWER OUTAGE

Now that the dry, hot months are here, there are nights when the entire city goes black. The electric lights go off, the music machine falls silent, the palm frond machine stops spinning and, for a moment, the whole city is still.

It feels like the end of the world.

If only it were.

NO REMEDY

I tuck Monica's little sock doll under my dress today and sneak down the hall to give it back to her, but as I round the corner, Shilpa catches me.

"Don't bother looking for your friend," she says. "She's out on the street."

Her words are thick and watery, the way they get when she has been drinking the liquor the street boy sells her. I wonder if I have misunderstood. I run to the window and look out on the street. There is the usual assortment of vendors, schoolchildren kicking a ball, a policeman smoking a cigarette. But no Monica.

"Where is she?" I say.

Shilpa shrugs. "Mumtaz has no use for her anymore."

"Why?" I say. "Monica was a good earner."

"Don't you know?" she says. "She has the virus."

In this city, there are many diseases and many remedies.
For the fever-and-chills disease, there are white pills. For the coughing disease, there is a special tea. For the itching and scratching disease, there is a golden ointment. For the burning pain in the groin, there is a shot from the dirty-hands doctor.

But for the virus, there is no remedy.

THE STREET BOY

I have been watching the street boy for some time now. I still do not buy his tea, but I no longer flee the room when he arrives.

I know that he lets Anita have her tea even if she doesn't have the money until the next day. I know that he puts extra sugar in the cook's tea in exchange for a stale heel of bread. And I know he sometimes cheats Mumtaz out of her change if she is not paying attention.

Each day I hear him coming, the sound of his teacups clattering in his caddy as he arrives at the kitchen door. And each day when he comes to our room, I turn my back so I will not be tempted to spend even a single rupee on a luxury I have learned to live without.

Today when he arrives, I am alone. He holds a cup of tea in my direction. The day is chilly and his tea is warm and fragrant, but I pretend I do not notice.

He lifts the cup to his lip and pretends to drink. "Some tea for you today?" he says. His brown eyes are dark as Tali's.

I shake my head no.

He lowers his head and scuffs one bare foot against the other. He seems about to say something more, but I turn my back, all the while thinking about his tea, about how good it would taste, how the cup would warm my hands, my throat, my whole being. And then he is gone, the cups on his caddy clinking and chattering as he retreats down the hall.

RAID

What I remember is this:

It was the middle of the afternoon. Shahanna was upstairs painting her nails, Mumtaz was out getting herself fitted for a new sari, and Anita and I were in the TV room with the other girls when there was thunder at the front door. A man's voice shouted, "Police!"

The goonda at the front door, a skinny boy Mumtaz hired just a few days ago, leaped to his feet and ran for the back door. The girls jumped out of their seats and scattered like roaches. I couldn't move.

Anita was running for the kitchen, but when she saw me frozen in place, she came back, grabbed my wrist, and pulled me along with her. The cook was waiting for us, holding open a panel beneath the sink. Anita crawled in first, then pulled me in behind her.

In the tiny dark space, there was barely enough room for one person, let alone two, and so once the door was shut, we huddled there amid the pipes and rags and buckets, holding our breath.

Soon we heard yelling. Men's voices came closer. Heavy footsteps coming toward us, down the hall, then into the kitchen. A man shouted at the cook. She cursed at him.

Cupboard doors were flung open and slammed shut. There was the sound of rice spilling, a pan clattering to the floor, the cook shrieking and stomping her foot.

The footsteps came close, then closer, and stopped.

Anita's hand found mine and we held on tight.

Then angry voices came from upstairs. I could hear furniture being overturned, wood splintering, a man yelling, a woman crying.

There was a stampede of footsteps, then running. And then the men were heading away from where we were hiding. Next came a heavy thud, a crash, then quiet.

After that, all we could hear was muttering and the shuffling of feet. Eventually the front door slammed shut.

When it was finally still, the cook came and opened the cupboard. I climbed out, but Anita refused to budge. When finally she crawled out, I could see that Anita had wet herself.

What I saw next was this: rice and lentils, flour and spices, enough food for a week, strewn about the floor, a pair of rats nibbling on the spoils as the cook fought with them for what remained. In the next room, the TV was dashed to the floor, its magic window now a hundred shards of glass.

I ran upstairs, saw our room in chaos, our beds overturned,
Anita's movie star posters ripped from the wall.

The worst is what I did not see: Shahanna.

AFTERMATH

When all the other girls come out of their hiding places, and the ones who ran down the lane come back, we all huddle in the TV room. The cook runs off to the sari shop to find Mumtaz.

"I bet it was the Americans," whispers Anita.

Shilpa spits. "It was the probably the police. Sometimes, they take a girl when Mumtaz falls behind in her payment."

I swallow and say nothing.

Mumtaz storms into the TV room, her fat mango face slick with sweat.

"Get to work, you lazy whores," she says.

When no one moves, she shoves Shilpa and she falls to the floor, nearly landing in a pile of broken glass.

"Clean up this mess," Mumtaz cries. "So we can be back in business tonight."

She doesn't say anything about Shahanna.
And when I dare to ask, the only answer comes from her leather strap.

GOSSIP

The next day at the morning meal, Anita says it was the Americans who took Shahanna away. The peanut vendor said he saw the whole thing. He told the cook and she told Anita.

"They probably stripped her naked and left her in the gutter," she says.

Shilpa says it was the police. A police officer who is one of her regular customers told her it was because Mumtaz didn't pay up this month.

"They probably beat her and left her for dead," she said.

I cannot stand to hear them talk about my poor, good friend, and so I rise and leave the table. The last thing I hear is one of them saying that we'll never know the truth.

I go up to my room, lie on my bed, and pull the thin blanket over my head, because I know at least one truth: if these terrible things have happened to Shahanna, it is all my fault.

IMMOBILE

Now that Shahanna is gone, Mumtaz says we must service her customers as well as our own.

I tell her I am ill, but the truth is that all I do is lie in bed and read Harish's beautiful American storybook over and over again.

And so Mumtaz sends the men up to me. They come, a parade of them, and I simply lie here unmoving.

TODAY

As I lie in bed this afternoon, I see a rat crawl out of the privy hole. He claws his way up the bedsheet, then scrabbles toward the crust of bread Anita must have left on my pillow.

We look each other in the eye for a moment. Then he runs away, my breakfast between his teeth.

ALL I HAVE LEFT

Anita says Mumtaz is going to sell me to another brothel. Her crooked face is wet with tears. She says that if I don't get up and join the other girls, I will be gone by nightfall.

"Please," she begs.

All I want to do is lie in my bed and repeat the beautiful American words from Harish's book, to say them over and over until one blends into the other, a chant that keeps all other thoughts away.

I can feel Anita shaking my shoulders and I can see her mouth moving in frantic pleas.
But her voice is far away.

All at once, there is a smack.

I hear it more than I feel it. Then, vaguely, I am aware of a smarting sensation on my cheek. And I understand that Anita has hit me.

I sit up, as if waking from a long sleep, and see this poor girl with the lopsided face. She is all I have left in the world.

I rise, shaky, as Anita helps me to my feet. She puts her arm around my waist and guides me toward the mirror. Then she gets out her makeup brushes and lip colors and paints my face with such tenderness that I think my heart will break.

A HIDING PLACE

The next day, as I am walking down the hall, I hear a voice coming from the closet. "Psst, Lakshmi," says someone. "In here."

I stop, open the door, and see Anita inside the shallow cupboard, her body flattened against the wall.

"Next time there is a raid," she says, "I'm going to hide in here."

"But, Anita," I say, "anyone can open this door."

She holds up a metal lock with numbers on its face.

"I stole it," she says, her crooked face half smiling, "from the grain bin."

I don't understand. Until she points to a hasp on the inside of the door.

"We can lock ourselves in," she says. "Then no one will be able to open this door."

ANOTHER AMERICAN

This one comes to the door looking somewhat lost. He is not as tall as the first one, and his eyes and hair are as dark as a normal man's, but my heart thuds when he points to me and he follows me up the steps.

I wait for him to shake my hand, but he just looks around the room. I wait for him to ask if I want to go to the clean place, but he fumbles through his pants pockets and mutters something in a language I cannot understand.

I know what to do. I lift the corner of the mat on the floor and feel around for the white card the other American gave me. I hold it out to him.

He looks puzzled. He sits down on the bed. He seizes my braid and pulls me down on top of him as the white card flutters to the floor.

It is then that I see the red veins in his eyes and smell the liquor on his breath.

He is not a good American. He is just another drunk.

CALCULATIONS

It has been more than two weeks since Shahanna left.
A new girl is sleeping in her bed, but I take no notice of her.
All I care about is my book of figures.

I pore over the book that shows all my careful penciled entries:
the money I've earned
and the money I've paid Mumtaz,
for makeup,
for nail paint,
for the rotten rice that is my daily dinner,
for my bed,
for the visits from the dirty-hands doctor.

Today I will show her my calculations, the figures I've
checked and rechecked and checked again, the numbers that
say I will have paid down my debt—by this time next year.

JUST A CUP OF TEA

The street boy is at my door again today. Again he holds out a cup of tea. And again I shake my head no.

I go back to my book of figures and wait for him to leave. But he crosses the room, places the tea on the little table next to my bed and, without saying a word, disappears.

A RECALCULATION

It is against the rules to speak to Mumtaz. It is Shilpa who does the talking for her. But I am standing outside the room where Mumtaz counts her money. Waiting.

I tap on her door frame.

"Shilpa? You miserable girl, get in here," she says.

I push aside the curtain and enter her darkened room.

She looks up, astonished. I say nothing. I simply hand her my ledger book.

She studies it, glancing up at me, then down at my calculations.

"You are a clever girl," she says.

I bite my lip.

"But you are forgetting a few things."

She gets out her own ledger book, with entries more copious than mine.

"The medicine I gave you," she says, licking the tip of her pencil.
"Your clothes . . .
The shoes on your feet . . .
The electricity bill."

She waves her hand toward the ceiling, where the fan
chugs dully.
"Who do you think pays for the comforts I provide?" she says.
"The fans? The music? The TV you girls love so much?
Do you think all that is free?"

I bite the insides of my mouth.

"And then there's interest," she says.
"You don't think I gave this money to your family for nothing
in return, do you?"

I dig my nails into my palms.

"Of course not!" she cries. "I charge half again as much for
interest."

I blink back the tears welling in my eyes.

"You are a clever girl, but not so clever, are you?" she says.

I simply stare at her.

"Let me do the calculations for you," she says.
She pretends to be adding and subtracting.
"Yes," she says. "It's as I thought. You have at least five more
years here with me."

ANY MAN, EVERY MAN

Here at Happiness House,
there are dirty men,
old men,
rough men,
fat men,
drunken men,
sick men.

I will be with them all.

Any man, every man.

I will become Monica.

I will do whatever it takes
to get out of here.

WHATEVER IT TAKES

I have a regular customer now.
He makes me do a nasty thing, but he gives me 10 rupees extra.

I had a drunken customer yesterday. When he fell asleep afterward, I went through his wallet and helped myself to 20 rupees more.

A deformed man came to the door yesterday. I told him I would be with him, for 50 rupees extra.

A WARNING

It is only midmorning, well before the customers usually arrive, but a wealthy man with fine clothes and a shiny gold watch has come to the door. It is too early for others to be awake, so I go to him and ask if he would like to be with me.

He looks me over.

I tell him I will make him happy.

He is considering this when Shilpa comes in and pushes me aside. Her eyes are wide and unblinking, the way they get when she has been drinking. She greets the man by name and wraps her arms around his thick waist. Then the two of them go to her room.

Later, when they are finished, she comes to my room. "Stay away from him, you understand?"

I understand that this wealthy man is one of her regulars. But I will not agree to what she asks. I will do what I have to do to get out of here. I shrug.

"Stay away from the ones that are mine, you hear me?" she says.

I used to fear Shilpa, but I look her in the eye. "No," I say.

"Not if it means a few extra rupees toward what I owe Mumtaz."

She spits. "You stupid hill girl," she says. "You actually believe what she's told you?"

I do. I have to believe.

MONSTER

A new girl arrived today. I know because I heard her sobs through the door of the locked-in room as I passed by on my way to the kitchen.

Mumtaz is a monster, I tell myself. Only a monster could do what she does to innocent girls.

But I wonder. If the crying of a young girl is the same to me as the bleating of the horns in the street below, what have *I* become?

PASSING THE TIME

Some days, the time between when I awake and the time when the customers arrive is so long and dull and tedious, that I can only lie in bed and watch the spinning of the palm frond machine.

These are the days when I understand Shilpa and the way she loves her liquor.

And so when the street boy comes today, I do not pretend I cannot see him. I look at his caddy and point to the bottle he has brought for Shilpa.

He shakes his head. "This is bad stuff," he says in my language. "Once you start it, you cannot stop."

"What do you care?" I say.

He looks down, fiddles with his wire caddy for a bit, then looks back at me, his dark brown eyes as wide and unblinking as Tali's. Then he takes a cup of tea from the caddy and holds it out to me. "Take this instead," he says.

I shake my head.

He turns to go, then stops. "I can bring you other things," he says. "I can bring you sweet cakes."

I sigh and try to remember the time when a sweet cake was

enough to make me happy. I turn my face to the wall. He leaves without making a sound, but I can tell from the aroma that fills the room that once again he has left me a cup of tea.

SUSPICION

Shilpa passes by my room with her gold-watch customer, and I try to remember what it was she said the other day when she warned me to stay away from him.

When I told her I would do whatever I could to pay my debt to Mumtaz, she said that I was stupid. Her words come back to me: "*You actually believe what she tells you?*"

I wonder. What can she mean?

Shilpa is Mumtaz's spy. She is the one who guards the door to her counting room. She is the one who seems to know Mumtaz's secrets.

I have seen Mumtaz's record book; I know how she cheated me. But I wonder. Does Shilpa know something I don't?

A COCA-COLA

The street boy is at my door again today. He is holding a bottle of Coca-Cola.

"For you," he says.

I am curious about this drink. The people who drink it on TV are happy when its tiny fireworks go off in their mouths.

"I have no money," I say to him.

"It's okay," he says.

I regard him with some suspicion. "Why are you giving this to me?"

He shrugs.

"And why do you give me tea without asking for anything in return?"

He kicks one bare foot against the other. "We are both alone in this city," he says. "Isn't that reason enough?"

He doesn't wait for my answer. He removes the cap, and the bottle hisses at us like an angry snake. I shy away from it until it has finished its hissing. Then I take the bottle from him and bring it to my mouth. Little bubbles—so tiny they cannot be seen—sneak out from the bottle and tickle my nose. I think

I will sneeze, but nothing happens. I take a sip. It is true! A dozen tiny fireworks go off on my tongue. I cannot help but smile.

The street boy is smiling, too.

Then Shilpa calls out to him from down the hall. "Get in here, you lazy boy," she cries.

He turns to go. "I can bring you other things, you know, whatever you like," he says. "I know everyone in this town."

I have no need for other things, I want to tell him. This small gift is more than enough.

PAYING A DEBT

Today the street boy shows up late. He scurries past my door, his eyes downcast. I call out to him and he peeks around the door frame. His brow is cut, his cheek swollen with a big purple bruise.

"What happened?" I say.

"The boss," he says, touching his face gingerly.

I ask him why his boss would do such a thing. "If I don't collect for all the drinks," he says. "Sometimes he takes it out on me."

We are both quiet for a moment. I open my mouth to tell him I am sorry at the same time he opens his to say it's okay, and then we are quiet again.

He turns to leave, and I see that his clothes are worn thin, that they are nothing but rags.
"Come back tomorrow," I say.

He looks puzzled.

But I do not tell him that I have decided to borrow from Mumtaz, just this once, so that tomorrow he doesn't have to face his boss empty-handed.

REVELATION

Shilpa is alone in the counting room when I get there. I tell her I want to borrow 40 rupees.

She spits. "You are even stupider than I thought."

I do not care what this drunken woman thinks of me. I just want enough to pay the street boy what I owe. "What do you care?" I say. "It is my money. My family won't miss a few rupees."

She laughs. "You think the money goes home to your family?" she says.

I tell myself she is talking nonsense, the nonsense that comes when she is drunk.

"Bimla may have given your family a little sum when you left home," she says. "But the rest—the money from the customers—goes to Mumtaz. Your family will never see one rupee more."

I put my hands to my ears, but still I can hear what she is saying.

"You will never pay off what you owe," she says. "Mumtaz will work you until you are too sick to make money for her. And then she will throw you out on the street."

I shut my eyes and shake my head from side to side. She is wrong. Because if she is right, everything I've done here, everything that's been done to me, was for nothing.

A KIND OF SICKNESS

It has been three days since I learned the truth from Shilpa. I ran from her, straight to my room, where I was sick to my stomach all day and night. For two days more I lay in bed, too wretched to move. But last night I rose from my bed, put on my makeup, and went back to work.

And today when the street boy comes, I will be ready. Today I will ask him if it is really true that he knows everyone in this town. And today I will show him the small white American card with the flying bird on it.

STUPIDITY

The street boy is standing in the kitchen, and all the girls are gathered around him. He says today is his last day.

"The boss is giving my route to a new boy," he says with a shrug.

The other girls tickle and kiss him and tell him they will miss him. The cook ruffles his hair with her hand, then slips him a piece of fresh bread. Anita takes a rupee note from her waistcloth, presses it into his palm and says good-bye. Shilpa asks if the new boy will bring her what she needs.

I look at him with frantic eyes. He says not to worry, it is not my fault.

He steps toward the kitchen door. My heart is pounding so hard I think it will burst from my chest. I do not think. I run to him and throw my arms around him.

The others cackle and bray.

"Stupid girl," Shilpa says. "She must be in love with him."

I do not care if she thinks I'm in love with him. I don't care if she thinks I'm a fool. Because I didn't just hug him. I whispered in his ear and slipped him the flying-bird card.

WAITING

More than a week has passed since I gave the street boy the flying-bird card. Each day the new boy comes in his place. The new boy is slow and surly. He does not joke with anyone, and he refuses to give out so much as a single teacup without getting his money first.

I ask if he ever sees the boy who used to bring us our tea.

"Who?" he says.

I realize then that I do not even know his name.

NOT A NEW GIRL ANYMORE

I look around the table at mealtime. There is a pair of new girls. One is sniffling over her rice and dal, the other is too dazed to eat. A third girl, one who has been here a while, is wiping her plate with her bread.

The first one is sitting in Monica's old seat, the second in Shahanna's. The third is sitting where Pushpa used to sit.

It occurs to me that, except for Anita, I have been here the longest.

COUGHING

I awake in the middle of the night to a familiar sound. It is the hacking of someone with the coughing disease. It took me a moment to realize, though, that Pushpa has long been gone. And a moment more to realize that this time, it is Anita.

DIGITAL MAGIC

It is only afternoon, but already a customer is at the door. I see at once that he is an American. It is not the same one who gave me the flying-bird card; this one is taller, and he is wearing a vest of many pockets. I shrink behind the door frame; every day I have prayed for an American to come. Now that one is here I don't know what to do.

I hear a noise from the counting room and see that Shilpa is watching. So I go to the man like a thirsty vine. I tell him I will make him happy. I tell him I know some good tricks.

Shilpa goes back to her movie star magazine, and the man follows me up the steps.

When we get to my room, he grips my hand in greeting, the same uncouth way the first American did. I pull away.

He says hello in my language. I say nothing in reply.

"What is your name?" he says. His words are hurried, and he looks nervously over his shoulder.

"Your name," he says again. "What is your name?"

I cannot open my mouth.

"How old are you?"

I don't reply.

He sighs. "May I take your picture?" he says. He takes a small silver box from one of his pockets. He touches a button and its eye blinks open with a whir.

I do not like this seeing box, but I do not object.

"I will not tell the fat woman," he says. "You have my promise."

A tiny lightning jumps out of the box, the eye blinks shut. And for a moment, I see doubles and triples of the man, framed in a red glow. He is smiling, looking at the back of his little lightning box.

"Come see your picture," he says.

I take just one step toward him and wait. He holds the silver box toward me, and I can see a tiny version of myself—smaller than the people on TV—in a tiny TV in the back of the silver box.

"Digital," he says.

I don't know this word, but it must be the name of the strange American magic he has that allows him to put me in his silver box.

"Do you want to leave here?" he says.

I cannot answer.
How do I know if he is a good man?
What if he is like the drunken American?
What if he is like the ones Anita talks about, the ones who make young girls walk naked in the street?

"I can take you to a clean place," he says. "Look," he says. "Pictures. Of the shelter. Other girls."

He holds out the silver box so I can see the tiny TV in the back.
He pushes a button.
There is a tiny image of a Nepali girl smiling back at me.
He pushes the button again.
There are girls in school uniforms sitting at a desk.
Girls fetching water at a spring.

The man turns off his digital magic machine. I am afraid, all of a sudden, that he is leaving. I wish there was a way to say something, to keep this American here a little longer.

I reach under my bed and pull out the American storybook, the one Harish gave me. I hold it out toward the American. He cocks his head to one side, puzzled.

I point to a picture. "*Elmo*," I say.

He nods slowly.

"*Ice cream,*" I say.

"Yes," he says. "Very good."

"*America.*"

The man smiles.

I do not mean to, but I am smiling at this queer-looking man, smiling and trembling at the magic—not of his digital image-taking box—but at the magic of a handful of nonsense words to keep him here a little longer.

BELIEVING

The American man whispers. His way of speaking my language is hurried now as he reads from a battered Nepali wordbook. I see that it has the image of the flying bird on its cover, and I say a silent prayer of thanks to the street boy whose name I will never know.

"What the fat woman does here to you is bad," he says. "Very bad."

I nod.

"She cannot force you to do these things," he says.

This American is not so magical after all, I decide.
He doesn't know about Mumtaz's leather strap.
And the goondas.
And the chain on the door.

"I will come back for you," he says. "I will come back with other men, good men, from this country—fathers and uncles who want to help—policemen who are not friends of Mumtaz. We will take you away from here."

This is too good to believe.

"You must believe me," he says.

I shut my eyes tight. I don't know what to believe. I believed that the stranger in the yellow cloud dress was taking me to the city to work as a maid. I believed that Uncle Husband would protect me from the bad city people. I believed that if I worked hard enough here at Happiness House, I could pay down my debt. And I believed it was all worth it for the sake of my family.

I am too afraid to believe him.

And so I am going to believe that this strange pink man is a dream, a cruel trick of the mind. I am going to believe that when I open my eyes he will be gone.

I count to 100.
Count to 100 again
and open my eyes.

He is still there, gripping his battered Nepali wordbook.

"The clean place," I say. "I want to go there."

NAMASTE

The American man says he will come back. He will return, he says, as soon as he can, with the other men and the good police officers who will force Mumtaz to let me go.

When he returns, I must go with him quickly, before the goondas can try to stop us.

He bows and says, "Namaste," the word in my language that means hello and good-bye.

And then he is gone, leaving me to wonder if he was really here at all.

READY

When no one is looking, I pack my bundle for my journey to the clean place and hide it under my bed.

What I am taking:
my American storybook,
a hair ribbon Shahanna left behind,
my notebook,
my old homespun skirt,
Monica's rag doll.

What I am leaving behind:
the makeup and nail paint Mumtaz made me buy,
the condoms under my mattress,
everything that happened here.

TWO KINDS OF STUPIDITY

It has been three days, and still the pink-skinned man hasn't returned with the good policemen.

How stupid I was to believe in him and his digital magic.

How stupid I am to keep believing.

FORGETTING HOW TO FORGET

I learned ways to be with men. I learned how to forget what was happening to me even as it was happening.

But ever since the pink-skinned man came here, with his pictures of the clean place,
I cannot remember those ways.

Now, while I wait for the American to return, and the men come to my bed,
I clench the sheets in my hands, for fear that I will pound them to death with my fists.
I grit my teeth, for fear that I will bite through their skin to their very bones.
I squeeze my eyes closed tight, for fear that I will see what has actually happened to me.

PLAYING THE FOOL

Five days have passed, and still there is no sign of the American.

Only a fool would keep waiting after five days.

A KIND OF ILLNESS

This ache in my chest is a relentless thing, worse than any fever.

A fever is gone with a few of Mumtaz's white pills.
But this illness has had me in its grip for a week now.

This affliction—hope—is so cruel and stubborn, I believe it will kill me.

PUNISHMENT

It is a simple kitchen sound, the grinding of spices with a wooden pestle. Sometimes it means nothing more than spicy stew for supper. But sometimes it means that the cook is readying the hot chili punishment for one of us. And then it is a sound that turns even the hardest woman here into a whimpering child.

Because it means that someone has crossed Mumtaz,
that Mumtaz will smear chilies on a stick and put it inside the girl, and that all of us will be awake through the night, listening to the girl moan.

Anita inches up next to the cook, but doesn't dare to ask.
"Mumtaz is furious," the cook says. "One of the girls has betrayed her."

My legs give way beneath me as the tender place inside me imagines the burn of the hot chili stick. And then I am sweating and pacing and quaking and trying to figure out how Mumtaz learned about the American. I am shivering and shaking and forming the words I will use to beg for mercy.

My stomach is heaving with fear as I hear the heavy thud of footsteps in the hall.
But when Mumtaz enters the room, I show her the face of a docile Nepali girl, a girl who will put up no fight.

She storms past me, and I flinch as the hem of her sleeve brushes my arm.

She pushes the cook aside, takes her stick, rolls it in the chili powder, and wheels around to face me.

I fall to the floor, kissing her feet and weeping.

She gives me a kick in the ribs, and all the air flies out of me in a *whoosh.*
Then she is gone.

Soon I hear a piteous wailing coming from the next room.
Anita bends over me.
"It is Kumari, the new girl," she says, stroking my hair. "She accepted a bangle bracelet from a customer."

My shameful heart rejoices that it is Kumari, not me, who is crying. But I wonder. If this is what Mumtaz did over a bangle, what would she do if she knew about my American?

I press my cheek to the coolness of the floor and close my eyes. When I open them I see Mumtaz's painted toes inches from my face. Anita's feet scurry away.

"You certainly act the part of the guilty one," Mumtaz says from above me.

What I feel next is the gritty sole of her shoe on the side of my head, gently at first, then with steady, gathering force, relentless, building pressure until her full weight is on me.

She grinds her foot, and the metal edge of my earring bites into the flesh of my ear.
But I do not cry out.

The seconds tick by.

Then, somehow, I am outside myself, marveling at this pain, a thing so formidable it has color and shape. Fantastic red, then yellow, starbursts of agony explode in my head.
Then there is a blinding whiteness, and then blackness.

Somehow, without warning, the pain is gone. A new pain takes its place as Mumtaz yanks on my braid and drags me to my feet.

We are eye to eye. I can smell the sour tang of her sweat.
"Have you done something for which you should be punished?" she says.

I don't answer.

She yanks on my braid. My scalp yelps with pain.
But I don't say a word.

"Have you done something wrong?" she says, spit gathering in the corners of her mouth.
"Tell me, you stupid little hill girl."

Mumtaz has called me a little hill girl. Which is, still, what I am.

I meet her gaze. "No, Mumtaz," I say. "I haven't."

She lets go of my hair, and it takes all my strength to keep my knees from giving way.

"Then put on your makeup," she says, "and get back to work."

I stay upright until she is gone. Only then do I slump to the floor and touch the side of my head. My earring comes off in my hand, bloodied, but intact. And I know then that my earlobe has been torn clear through.

I know something else as well. I know that I would endure a hundred punishments to be free of this place.

THE WORDS HARISH TAUGHT ME

It is so late at night it is almost morning, and I am awake,
ready to begin another day of waiting for the American.
There is a banging on the door and a voice shouts, "Police!"

Anita bolts out of bed.
"Hurry," she says, grabbing my hand.

I am right behind her, sneaking down the hall toward her
hiding place in the closet.

We can hear voices coming from downstairs as we tiptoe
down the hall.

"I am here for a young girl," says a man.

"What kind of place do you think this is?" says Mumtaz.
"There are no young girls here."

I know this voice. It is my American.

I squeeze Anita's hand.
"It is an American," I whisper.

Her eyes go wide.

"He is a good man," I say. "He will take us to a clean place."

"It's a trick," she says, inching toward the closet.

"No," I say. "I've seen pictures. The girls there are safe."

She shakes her head.
"They are liars," she says. "I beg you. Don't go."

The American is shouting something. I don't understand what he is saying, but I know, somehow, that he is calling out to me.

"Please," I beg her. "Come with me. If you stay here, you will die."

Anita is clutching my arm. "Don't go," she cries.

I cannot move.
I cannot go to my American.
And I cannot walk away from my crooked-faced friend.

"The new TV is coming any day now," she says. "Mumtaz promised."
She grips my arm and tries to pull me into the closet with her.

I shake my head.

Then, slowly, she lets go of my arm, closes the door between us, and I hear a sad and final sound: the lock sliding into place.

I am alone in the hallway.

Mumtaz is cursing downstairs. But I can still hear the American.

I inch toward the steps. But I am too afraid to go down.

The American calls out.

I try to answer, but nothing comes out of my mouth.

I hear more cursing and the scuffle of feet. He is leaving.
My American is leaving.

Something inside me breaks open, and I run down the steps. I see Mumtaz, her fat mango face purple with rage, her arms pinned behind her back by two policemen. She lunges in my direction and spits. But the policemen hold her back.

I see my American. There are other men with him, Indian men, and the American lady from the picture.

"*My name is Lakshmi,*" I say.
"*I am from Nepal.*
I am fourteen years old."

AUTHOR'S NOTE

Each year, nearly 12,000 Nepali girls are sold by their families, intentionally or unwittingly, into a life of sexual slavery in the brothels of India. Worldwide, the U.S. State Department estimates that nearly half a million children are trafficked into the sex trade annually.

As part of my research for *Sold*, I traced the path that many Nepalese girls have taken—from remote villages to the red-light districts of Calcutta. I also interviewed aid workers who rescue girls from brothels, provide them with medical care and job training, and who work to reintegrate them into society.

But most touching and inspiring was interviewing survivors themselves. These young women have experienced what many people would describe as unspeakable horrors. But they are speaking out—with great dignity.

Some go door-to-door in the country's most isolated villages to explain what really happens to girls who leave home with strangers promising good jobs. Some of them—even women who are ill with HIV—patrol the border between Nepal and India on the lookout for young girls traveling without their parents. And some are facing their traffickers in court—where it is often their word against the fathers and brothers, husbands and uncles who sold them for as little as three hundred dollars.

It is in their honor that this book was written.

ACKNOWLEDGMENTS

I am deeply grateful to my patient, wise, and gifted editor, Alessandra Balzer, who raised the bar ever so gently, every time she read this manuscript, and to my tireless and enthusiastic agent, Nina Collins, who believed in this book from the first word. I'm also grateful to all the talented and energetic people at Hyperion, especially Angus Killick, who are indefatigable in their efforts to get books into the hands of readers who need them.

I owe a special debt of thanks to my wise and generous colleagues—Mark Millhone, Andrea Chapin, Rachel Cohn, Mark Belair, A.M. Homes, Chris Momenee, and Mo Ogrodnik—who were every bit as invested in this story as I was. And to Annie and Steven Pleshette Murphy, Bridget Starr Taylor, Chris Riley, Joan Gillis, Patricia and Donald Oresman, Hallie Cohen, and Bill Ecenbarger, who read this manuscript at various stages and who gave honestly and generously of their feedback and friendship.

This book could not have been written without the help of Ruchira Gupta and Anuradha Koriala, who paved the way for me to visit the Maiti Nepal shelter for women and children in Kathmandu; the village of Goldhunga in the Himalayas; the Apne Aan women's center in Calcutta; and the Deepika Social Welfare Center for Women and Children in the red-light district of Calcutta. I'm also grateful to P.L. Singh, G.P. Thapa, and Harish Rao, who guided me on my travels, and to Luna Ranjit, who fact-checked this book so diligently. My deepest thanks go to the real Shahanna, who was my guardian angel in the red-light district of Calcutta, and who gave me her strength and wisdom when I needed it most.

I am also grateful to the New York Foundation for the Arts for its award of a fellowship in support of this project.

Most of all, I am grateful to my family—Meaghan and Matt, Brandon and Kelly, and, of course, Paul—who shows me the power of love to change everything.